THE TROUBLE WITH ORDER

FAIRYLAND ROMANCES BOOK 5

JAXON KNIGHT

Cover by Kat Savage

ISBN kindle edition 978-0-473-57045-3

Paperback 978-0-473-57044-6

Published by Grey Kelpie Studio

❀ Created with Vellum

Dedicated to Will Howard, my adopted little brother. Thanks bro,
Treasure the Unicorn loves you and I do too.

LINK WINKED AT THE SECURITY GUARD WHO HAD BEEN FOLLOWING him around as he did a circuit of the Enchanted Forest, indicating he was ready to knock off and head back. He couldn't wear a watch as Fairy Mischief, and although sometimes he could sneak a look at someone's phone as they took a selfie, it wasn't really cool to ask the time. He figured he'd done about an hour and a half out, which was plenty, especially since it was unseasonably warm for February.

The security guard, Francisco, nodded slightly in response, and Link headed towards the big tree housing the changing rooms the fairy characters used.

On the way, he spotted a family group who looked a bit harassed. The two littlest kids were fussing and crying, clearly tired out, the young teen was deep in their phone paying no attention, and the mother was hunting through a backpack, trying to find something while the father studied the map of the park as if his life depended on it.

Link changed direction and waved at the group. One of the little kids, stuffed into a puffy Treasure the Unicorn jacket and possibly overheating, stopped grizzling and looked up with wet eyes.

"Faiwy Misjif?"

"That's me!" Link beamed and went down on one knee, so the

kids didn't have to look up too much. They were little, maybe not yet five years old. "What's your name?"

"Jeff!" the other one pushed forward, he was wearing a matching jacket but it was the Sparkles the Dragon version.

"And I'm Jonny."

"Pleased to meet you both, how are you liking the Enchanted Forest?" Link glanced up to see the father had pulled out his phone to take photos. He gave him a subtle nod to encourage him.

"It's big!" Jeff said, a hint of the whine coming back.

"It's pretty," Johnny asked.

"Thanks, it's my house, so I'm glad you think it's pretty. What all have you two been doing?"

"The spinning lily pads," Johnny said.

"Over and over and over," the teen grumbled. Link caught their eye and gave his most winning smile. He knew that his social media presence was big because of teens like this one who related to him, and his being good looking certainly helped as well. The teen almost smiled. Almost.

"Say, I don't suppose you know where the restaurant is?" The father butted in. It wasn't an unusual question, but sometimes it irked Link when people phrased things like this, he was supposed to stay in character and be an exciting experience for the kids, not give directions. But on the other hand, it was more than clear that this family really needed a sit down and some food.

"The Forest Kitchen? Oh I love it there, it's up that way," he pointed, and then stood up. "Tell you what, I'll walk you there, because sometimes the paths in this place get a little confusing if you're not used to it. Would you like that, Jeffy and Johnny?"

"Oh my god, if you could that would be a godsend," the mother said, her voice tense but relieved.

"Then it's decided." Link grinned and did a little spin in place, to bring some lightness to the situation.

The twins giggled and nodded, and instantly took his hands. "Yes! Will you have dinner with us too?"

"Oh, I can't stay for dinner," he said. "But thank you so much for asking! There's a big party at Fairy Gentle's tonight, and I have to be there. If I don't go, no one will swap the cupcakes for daisies and the roses for cupcakes."

Once the family had been escorted to the Enchanted Forest Kitchen and Link had taken a few photos with them, he and Francisco used the discreet gate into the staff only area of the Forest and went to the changing room.

It was more modest than the Airlock, the large one the princes, princesses and fursuit characters used. The fairies simply didn't need as much storage space for their costumes, and it was nice to have a private area just for the fairies.

Set in a large fake tree, and commonly referred to as 'the Treehouse', the changing rooms opened with the swipe of a security pass, and inside were two rooms. The thin, narrow one you walked right into was the entrance, where people did their last touch ups and gathered before going out into the park.

In behind was the changing room, just one for all genders, in a curious O shape. In the centre of the room was a wide pillar with mirrors and small shelves attached, so actors could get their makeup on. The outer rim of the room was lined with couches and racks of costumes, alternating, with a space for each named character. As there were generally only one or two fairies rostered on at a time the lack of space wasn't a problem, and the actors were all good enough friends that no one minded the shared changing space.

He went straight for his phone and shot off a message to Cillian.

L: Kills, I miss your stupid scoundrel face, let's hang out soon

No response. In fact, Cillian had been too busy to hang out for almost a week now. Link missed him although he tried not to. He set his phone down and sighed, then realized he'd missed a note pinned to the rack holding his costumes. He got up to read it.

Link, come see me at my office before you go, something new's come up, Lennon.

For a moment, Link's heart thumped unpleasantly at being

summoned to Lennon's office like that, but he dismissed the fear. He had nothing to worry about, he was good at his job and there was no chance of Fairy Mischief being phased out.

Besides they'd mentioned 'something new' which was hardly 'you're in trouble and about to be fired'.

He sat on the plush couch beside his rack of costumes and took a deep drink from his water bottle. His shift was due up in an hour, and most of that was wind-down time, time to remove make up thoroughly, get changed and so on. Then, when he went into the park no one would recognize him. He'd rest a moment, then get changed and head over to the Airlock to see Lennon.

Soon he was dressed in civvies: jeans, sneakers, a ballcap with the Fairyland logo on it, and a Davey Typhoon T-shirt his best friend Cillian had given him for Christmas and insisted he wear. The joke being of course, that Cillian played Davey in the park, and was always making fun of Link for being a fairy. Link had, of course, got him the sparkliest, most over the top Fairy Mischief hoodie for Christmas, because they loved making the same jokes.

It was a quick walk down the staff only paths through the trees to the Airlock, and Link let himself in, eying the vending machine briefly, but Lennon was in their office with the door open so he hurried in.

"Afternoon boss," Link said, plonking himself down in the visitor's chair. "What's up?"

"Hello, Lincoln," Lennon said, being weirdly formal even though the note had been addressed to him by his common name. "Thanks for making time to see me."

"Of course."

"I wanted to inform you that there's a number of new recruits on their way in. Starting next week, on Max Jones's orders. Since after Valentine's Day there's a bit of a lull theme wise, he's expanded our roster of character actors."

"Oh?" Link smiled. It would be nice to have some more fairies and animals and things around. It always added so much value to the atmosphere, in Link's opinion.

"Indeed." Lennon pushed a mockup of a flyer towards him. It was purple and green and had the word 'Villains' emblazoned across it. Underneath, some sketches of characters he knew from the Fairyland movies. The bad guys... including... yep. Lord Order. The bad guy Fairy Mischief came up against... his curiosity peaked and then dipped again. His mouth went dry. What did this mean for him?

"The villains?"

"Yes, I believe Max wants a little more drama in some of the parades and shows. You know more than anyone that there's some appeal in the less... how shall I put this?" Lennon tapped their lower lip and looked past Link to where the doors with little crowns on them were. "Less righteous characters. Obviously, the princes and princesses are well loved, but market research shows the villains are popular as well."

"Sure," Link looked over the pamphlet once more and then handed it back. "So, I guess I'll be what? Sword fighting with the new guy out in the park?"

Lennon smiled. "Perhaps, well, maybe not actually fighting with weapons. But there will be some new scripted shows and some new floats in the parade perhaps, specially themed. We expect them to be ready in a month."

Scripted shows? That's a bit of a change to what I usually do, which is just wander around and improv.

"Cool, and you said they're in next week?"

"That's right," Lennon said. "I called you in because we're running a new kind of training for them. Since you and the person playing Lord Order will be working so closely together, same with the others who have their villains cast now, we'll need you to come in every day next week for training alongside them."

"Oh?" Link mentally checked his calendar but it had been woefully empty lately, and remained so for the foreseeable future. "Should be fine."

"So, if you'd like to take the rest of this week off, that's fine. Or you can work just some of your shifts, whatever works best for you."

"I'll work tomorrow and then take the rest of the week," Link said. "Money's always good, but some downtime would be nice too. I could get some surfing in."

"That's fine. Oh, and since you mentioned money, here," Lennon smiled and pushed an envelope towards Link. "It's a significant change to your job, so there's a pay raise attached, for the duration of the trial. We'll negotiate a little more when the trial is over and we know more about how the job will look."

Link took the envelope and slipped it into his jacket, although desperate to check the amount, it felt a little rude to tear it open right there. "Thanks, that's great. Uh, so who all else is involved?" Link said.

"Princess Constance and Witch Faithless, Princess Patience and Wizard Haste, although we might trade Ariana out for Nate, I'm not convinced on that one... and Fairy Gentle and the Bad Fairy Coldness. Four pairs, all up."

Link nodded. "Cool, okay, will be nice to work with some people closely, I guess." He didn't sound convinced even to himself but Lennon didn't seem to mind.

"All right, make sure you file all your hours over the next few days and we'll be starting Monday morning nine am, out back here. My new assistant, Arlo, will be your contact person."

2 / TAEYANG

THE FAIRYLAND CONTRACT WAS THOROUGH, AND TAEYANG appreciated their attention to detail. He'd signed it, and sent it back, and called his parents back in South Korea to let them know he had a "proper" regular job.

They knew about theme parks, at least, because they'd been to some of the bigger ones in Seoul and on their trip to Japan. They sat side by side on their old couch and smiled at him over the video call.

"It's good that you have a regular job," his mother said. "We worry about you, Tae."

"I know," he said. "But I'm actually fine, even with the irregular work I was doing before."

"This is a good opportunity for you," his father said. "You must send us pictures of you in your costume."

Taeyang laughed and nodded. "Of course I will."

The days between sending in the contract and starting on Monday morning flew by and soon he was driving in, taking a space in the staff parking lot and making his way in through security. A tall woman with long blond hair approached the security booth at the same time, and it turned out she was a new recruit as well.

"Lily Ysabel. Not Lily, Lily Ysabel thank you," she said. Then she grinned, showing perfectly white, even teeth. "I'm playing the wicked witch."

The man at security looked up at her and grinned, checking her name off a piece of paper on a clipboard. "I bet you are. I'm Cody, I'm head of security for the day shift. And you are?" he turned to Taeyang, and Lily Ysabel did too, an eyebrow arched.

"Taeyang Park," he said. "I'm Lord Order."

"Cool," Cody checked his name off as well. "I'll lead you two over to the training center. All four of you starting today will go through processing together, get your IDs and stuff. Then it's right into training from what Lennon said."

"Thanks." Taeyang gave Lily Ysabel a smile and she returned it, rolling her eyes a little.

"Feels a little weird starting as a bad guy, doesn't it?"

He chuckled and nodded. "A little, but I'm looking forward to it. Bad guys are more fun to play, in my experience."

Cody turned and led them through into the park proper. It was pleasantly empty and felt a lot tidier for not having people inside it.

Taeyang felt a thrill of excitement as Cody led them to a gate with a staff only sign on it and ushered them through. He wasn't a huge Fairyland fan like some were, but he wasn't immune to the glamor of it either.

Although perhaps glamor isn't the right word, he thought, as the path wound through slightly overgrown underbrush to the corporate looking building with large windows in front. *Exciting yes, but this building looks like the kind of place people would come for cut price corporate retreats.*

They walked through the hallway space and down to a back room, it was large and smelled vaguely like a gymnasium. There were two people standing at a table, one Taeyang recognized from the interview - Lennon, who seemed to be a very hands on manager who handled a lot of things, and a young man with a fresh face, tightly curled almost brown hair and a pale complexion.

"Lennon, Arlo, these are two of your new recruits," Cody said.

"I'm heading back to the front gate now, and I'll bring the others when they arrive."

"Welcome," the young man, who had to be Arlo, said. He came forward with a clipboard in each hand and handed them to Taeyang and Lily Ysabel. "I'm Arlo, I'm going to be coordinating all your training this week. It's great to meet you." He hesitated slightly, then grinned. "You're Taeyang and Lily Ysabel, perfect casting, really."

Taeyang took the clipboard and smiled. "Thank you, I'm very excited to be here."

"Once the other two are here, we'll get you all sorted with IDs and then get into training." Lennon said, they gestured at the seats lining one wall. "Feel free to take a seat. The character actors you're being paired with will be here to train alongside you. They're all veterans who've worked at the park for at least a year, so you'll have lots to learn from them, and they'll support you all through the process."

Taeyang felt a nervous flutter at that, being paired up with a 'veteran' character actor as he learned was a great idea, he'd have a proper mentor who understood what was required and how to act and everything.

But at the same time it was intimidating. He had done a little Instagram stalking of his opposite, the man who played Fairy Mischief, and he was very good at his job. He had the expressions down, a handsome, flirtatious but still innocent and non-threatening air to him. He was very popular and a lot of people seemed to love him. He swallowed and sat down in the seat, Lily Ysabel sat beside him and crossed her legs.

The last new recruits were ushered in when Taeyang was part way through filling in his form. They were all introduced to each other.

The man playing Wizard Haste was a striking man called Stefan and Phoenix James was the handsome person playing Bad Fairy Coldness.

"I don't like pronouns," Phoenix James said. "None of them mean anything to me, so just use whatever ones you'd like. Or my name, for preference. My name, which, by the way is Phoenix James, both words, because there are just too many James' in the world."

Taeyang made a mental note to use they/them pronouns for Phoenix James, same as Lennon used. "Nice to meet you, I'm Taeyang Park. I use he/him pronouns," Taeyang said, shaking hands with each of the new introductions.

"Great, now that everyone's here, I'll go and fetch the others," Arlo said. He left with a distinct bounce in his step.

"Taeyang, is that a Korean name?" Stefan asked, his smile mildly interested.

"It is. I was born in South Korea, and I moved here for high school when I was twelve."

"Amazing," Stefan said. "My family's Polish but we moved here together when I was a kid. I love Korean pop music."

"Okay?" Taeyang was a bit surprised by this sudden admission but at least it appeared to be a kind one.

The door opened again and people started to file in. It was easy to guess who was cast in which role, as the likenesses were all so good.

And there's Fairy Mischief, walking in like he owns the place.

Instead of introducing them all to each other, Arlo got them all to introduce themselves and their roles, and it was just as awkward as any team building event Taeyang had ever attended.

"Hi, I'm Nate, and I play Prince Valor." Nate raised his hand and gave a smile that almost looked shy. "I guess I'll be working with Wizard Haste, Ari will be too, she's Princess Patience, but for now it's just me. She's got some stuff going on in her life, so I'll do the first lot of this stuff while she keeps on at her normal job." Taeyang liked how humble Nate seemed to be. Of course, this was the same man who had jumped into the lake in full prince costume to rescue a little girl who'd fallen in. It would have been easy to let that go to his head, Taeyang imagined, but he seemed a bit uncomfortable with everyone looking at him.

"Hi! I'm Lincoln Miller, I play Fairy Mischief. Great to have all you newbies here, I guess." Lincoln waved and smiled and Taeyang could practically smell the arrogance rolling off him.

He was even more handsome in real life than he was in the pictures. His strawberry blond hair had a soft natural wave to it and his eyes were bright. Taeyang knew there was almost no chance he had a dusting of glitter over his cheeks, but the freckles there somehow gave the illusion of it.

Knows how handsome he is. I bet he's a horrible boyfriend.

Wait, why am I thinking about him as a boyfriend at all? Ridiculous.

A soft spoken woman with warm brown skin and long curly hair waved next. "I'm Fairy Gentle," she said. "Real name Rosa, welcome to Fairyland everyone."

"And that just leaves me, Julia," the last woman said. She also had long brown hair but she wasn't smiling as warmly as Rosa. "I play Princess Constance. I guess they might be using Grayson, uh, Magnificence as well? But I'm here for now."

Thankfully, then Arlo invited them to sit down and listen to Max Jones. They dragged over folding chairs. Taeyang set his alongside Lily Ysabel's, setting up a pretty clear straight line for others to follow, but Lincoln, the man who played Fairy Mischief didn't seem to notice and shoved his chair down at an angle and out of the imaginary line Taeyang had started. The others set their chairs down haphazardly after that, and Taeyang tried very hard not to let it get to him.

He eyed Link and wondered if he'd done it on purpose. Taeyang was there to play Lord Order after all, and Fairy Mischief's entire *raison d'être* was to foil Lord Order's careful ways.

Almost like Mischief is the villain, Taeyang thought fleetingly. But he dismissed it. He wasn't there to subvert the character after all.

Max walked in then, which was a welcome reprieve from his own thoughts.

Max Jones was a handsome man and well turned out in a black designer suit over a pale lavender shirt with a darker purple tie. He had an easy smile which made Taeyang feel more comfortable.

"Thanks all, and welcome to Fairyland for those who are new. I don't want to take up too much of your time here, but Lennon thought it was important that you hear my vision directly from me. So, you may be aware that I'm looking seriously into park expansions, adding another themed area, but that's going to take time, obviously. I can buy the land but I can't just wave my magic wand and have new attractions appear overnight, I mean. Unfortunately." He rolled his eyes and the assembled actors gave a polite laugh.

"So, while we wait for that to happen, I had this idea to introduce some new characters and have a little fun with encounters and make believe, really engage our guests and give them something unexpected. Hence, our new friends, who will also be our new villains."

He explained his ideas for how things could work with regards to shows, scripted scenes in the park, parades and meet and greets. Taeyang paid attention with one ear but kept finding his attention wandering to Lincoln, who didn't seem to be listening at all.

3 / LINK

"THIS ISN'T A NEW IDEA, THOUGH." MAX JONES CONTINUED. "THOSE who've been around a while will know that over in Pirate's Cove we've had huge success for years with Mary Rose Magellan and Davey Typhoon, as well as the other pirates. They've always been hugely popular, so in some ways we're just expanding that out to the rest of the park."

Link resisted the urge to check his phone again. He wanted to look at it very badly. He could feel it vibrating in his pocket with each new message sent to the apartment's group chat. But he couldn't check it, he had to pay attention to Max Jones, and listen and do his job which he was being paid for.

But the phone kept on vibrating silently against his leg. *Should have just left it in the changing room.*

The last message he'd seen posted in the chat was from Roxy, saying she was moving out. It wasn't exactly a surprise to Link, she'd been getting serious with her girlfriend and had been spending more and more time over at her place instead of at the apartment. But the fact that the thread appeared to be blowing up was concerning. Did that mean others were angry with her? Were they talking about how to find someone new to take her room? Or the worst possible reason: were others talking about moving out as well?

He didn't know, and he couldn't check and it was awful.

Finally Max Jones asked if there were any questions, which meant he had to be wrapping up. Link looked at the others in their folding chairs and prayed no one would have any questions.

"I have one, actually," Taeyang said. He was the one playing Lord Order, and of course he had a question. He was already bamboozling Link and he wasn't even in character, technically.

"Sure, go ahead." Max said. "You're playing Lord Order, right?"

"That's right, I'm Taeyang," Taeyang said. "I was wondering about the possibility of improvisation in these scenes. I understand that to start with it will largely be scripted, but won't the guests get used to that quite quickly?"

Link frowned and picked at the rip in the knee of his jeans with his short fingernails.

Of course they'd be allowed to improvise, they just had to prove they knew the characters, first. Duh.

"Once we're sure you're comfortable in your characters," Lennon said, stepping up beside Max. "Then we're happy for you to improvise as long as you keep it clean and Fairyland friendly."

"Thank you," Taeyang said. "How soon do you expect us to be out in the park?"

Link suppressed a sigh of annoyance. That was clearly something Lennon would know, they could let Max Jones go and they'd all be able to relax but no, Taeyang had to ask all the questions.

I'm getting seriously annoyed with this guy. I guess it'll make my performance as his enemy more compelling.

Finally, Max Jones was leaving the room and Link pulled his phone out. A quick scan of the messages showed his worst fears were going to be realized. His roommates were all moving out.

His stomach sank. There was no way he could afford the apartment on his own, and with this new initiative happening at work it severely cut into his time to find new roommates. He'd have to put up a list and then vet people and meet them and decide if he could live with them or not.

Urgh it'd be such a drag.

The others were milling around and he realized Lennon was shaking hands and excusing themself, Arlo was directing people to the nearest restrooms.

"We'll start up again in ten!" He said.

Link leaned back in his folding chair and read the chat thread again, paying more attention this time. It was true, it was all really happening. They were talking about telling the landlord. *Better say something, I guess...*

But what? I can't afford the place on my own. Do I want to move as well? It's work to find a place just as much as it's work to find people to move in with me. I hate decisions.

Link: Hey guys, wow this is some big news. Um. Congrats Roxy on your relationship I guess. So everyone's going??

Roxy: thanks, boo!

Liam: yeah, we're all going, sorry :(Sad to break up the place but it looks like it's time.

Roxy: you can strike out on your own, Linkie

Link: yay?

Liam: come on, all those Fairyland big bucks, you can probably get a really nice place

Link's stomach turned over unpleasantly.

Yeah, the Fairyland big bucks... the ones I can never quite manage to save any of...

He looked up from his phone, not really seeing any of the others, and tried to think about where his money went. Well, his car was a stinker, it ate gas like, he didn't even know what it ate gas like. Like a hungry pig at dinner time. So, he was always buying gas and fixing his car, so there was that.

Then he liked to keep up to date with the newest Fairyland apparel, especially if it was Fairy related... And then there was food, because he only really knew how to cook three things and he was usually too tired after work to do that so he'd pick up takeaways or order in. Bills for the apartment on top of all that, plus the charity he donated to.

Well, he couldn't just stop donating to the kid's hospital. And there were other things as well, little things chipped away… an in-app purchase here and there on his favourite mobile games, new downloadable content on his console games, it all added up.

His stomach rumbled in a sort of menacing way and he shut down the apartment chat. He could deal with all of that later. For now, he had a job to concentrate on. He locked his phone, stood up and went to mingle.

4 / TAEYANG

THE TRAINING STARTED OUT WITH SOME VERY BASIC 'GETTING TO know you' games and the group moved around the room, everyone getting some time with each other until Arlo insisted they pair up with their in character partner. Taeyang spotted him nearby and went to stand beside him. Lincoln had been texting all through the break and didn't seem to have the cheer and sparkle Fairy Mischief usually did.

Taeyang eyed him, while Lincoln's gaze was fixed on Arlo.

"All right, since these are the people you're going to be spending a lot of your time with, now's your chance to really go deep." He was handing out pieces of paper to everyone. Taeyang looked at the two he'd been given. *'What would constitute a perfect day for you?'* the first one said. The second read *'When did you last sing to yourself?'*

"These questions you've been given," Arlo said, raising his voice to be heard over the murmuring of the group. "They're scientifically proven to deepen your relationship with the person you're talking to. The theory goes that this psychologist came up with thirty six questions and if you sit with someone and ask each other each one, and answer them honestly, that you can't help but be in love with them at the end of it. Now, I'm not going to insist you do all of the thirty six questions," he said.

A few people laughed.

"You *don't* want us all to fall in love?" Stefan asked, making a joke out of it. There were a few more laughs, and Taeyang chuckled as well.

"Not so much," Arlo said. "Although from what I've heard about this park's track record, it might just happen anyway."

Taeyang felt his lip curling and quickly schooled his face into a blank expression. He wasn't at all adverse to falling in love, but dating someone who you also worked with sounded complicated, and complicated things got very messy if they fell apart. He turned his gaze to Lincoln and couldn't begin to imagine falling in love with him. He was handsome for sure, gorgeous even, but he seemed disaffected. His attention was not truly on what was happening here. Taeyang was new at the job, and of course wanted to impress, he had the fresh energy of the new and hadn't been jaded by working at the park for a long time. But Lincoln's experience shouldn't have meant he wasn't open to new ideas.

"Get to it," Arlo said. "Ask the questions on your prompts of your partner, and both of you should try your best to answer honestly. Once that's done, and I'll give you twenty minutes or so, you'll share with the group what you learned about your partner."

Taeyang suppressed a groan and turned to face Lincoln properly. Lincoln did the same, and the air of reluctance coming from him was palpable. Taeyang figured he wouldn't wait for Lincoln to initiate anything.

"How about you start with one of your questions, Lincoln?"

"Just Link is fine."

"All right." Taeyang raised his eyebrows, prompting him to start. Lincoln sighed and looked down at his cards.

"Uh, okay, what roles do love and affection play in your life?" Lincoln pulled a face. "That's kind of a deep cut isn't it? I mean, I'm single and very aware of it."

"Perhaps it could mean other kinds of love?" Taeyang suggested. He tipped his head back to look at the ceiling for a moment. "My parents are both overseas, in Korea, so it's pretty distant. We video call sometimes but I guess I miss them a little?" He looked at Lincoln again.

"And how about affection?" Lincoln asked. Taeyang could see he was more focused now, more interested in what Taeyang was saying. Taeyang felt a little flutter of pleasure from his attention, which was ridiculous.

"I guess I don't have a lot of that," Taeyang admitted. "I'm single, too."

Lincoln frowned in sympathy. "Okay, so we're both lonely. My parents are nearby at least, a couple of hours drive with traffic, and I love my sister, but I don't see them as much as I'd like to."

"Is your sister older or younger?" Taeyang asked.

"Older," Lincoln replied. "By four years. Now you ask one of yours."

"Right. Uh, what would constitute a perfect day for you?" He asked. It felt so stilted, so scripted, like they were appearing on a television dating show from the sixties. But he wasn't sure how to actually connect, break through whatever this wall Link...Lincoln was putting up.

What was it? Nonchalance? A genuine dislike for what we're doing, or for me in particular? I've felt annoyed with him a few times already this morning. Perhaps I'm projecting that without meaning to. All right, deep breath and relax.

Taeyang took a deep breath, let go of the irritation he was feeling and gave Lincoln a smile. "What does your other one say?"

He puffed his cheeks out and puffed some air out as he read the card. "Do you feel your childhood was happier than most other people's?'

Taeyang curled his lip. "I kind of hate that question," he said, candidly. Lincoln looked relieved.

"Same, it's totally invasive, right? Like, what is happy? And it kind of puts you at a disadvantage if you had any kind of mental health issues or a parent died or something."

Taeyang felt a thrill of concern for Lincoln then, because yeah, it would absolutely be awful to have something like that happen when you were a kid, and to have to bring it up in a work setting, for the purposes of team building was horrible.

"I'm so sorry," Taeyang said, quickly. "You don't have to answer."

"Oh, it's actually fine," Lincoln said. "My parents are both still happily married and my childhood was pretty... fine. I mean I was sick quite a bit with asthma, but it was fine, I always got the treatment I needed. I just hate the thought of comparing it to others and being like yeah I was objectively happier than you were." He cracked a rueful smile. "You know?"

Taeyang cleared his throat, feeling off footed - he had been so ready to commiserate or try to soothe Lincoln but instead he was charmed by his smile. He had a chaos to him which was unsettling.

"Right, yes. I don't think I'd ever consider that my childhood was happier than most. I mean, we had enough to eat and a house and everything but..." He shook his head, not wanting to think of the arguments he'd had with his parents. The insisting on applying for school in the United States. "Never mind."

"Guess we're done then," Lincoln said. "Got enough to report back on, do you think?"

Taeyang nodded. "Yes."

5 / LINK

THE DAY PASSED IN A BLUR FOR LINK, DISTRACTED AS HE WAS BY THE thought of having to find somewhere new to live.

The question about childhood had made him think of his folks. They'd take him in if he was in desperate need, but they lived so far from Fairyland he'd have to give up his job. The commute would be killer.

And then Mom would be fussing over me, making sure I was staying warm and safe and panicking every time I coughed or cleared my throat. Never mind I haven't had anything worse than a slight wheeze in years. She can never stop seeing me as that sick kid...

And on top of that, he'd then be the loser who lived with his folks and had no job. He couldn't bear the thought of that. Not when he'd made such a good job of being Fairy Mischief.

He finished up the day feeling like his skin didn't fit. If he'd just been allowed to have a normal work day, playing with kids and posing for photos and climbing trees... he'd be able to face all his problems, he was sure of it.

But instead he'd had to try to make nice with a man who sneered at him, and was weirdly cold. He was in some ways glad that he and Taeyang hadn't instantly bonded. It would be odd to play against someone he genuinely liked, so at least the casting would work in his favour that way. But on the other hand, how was he supposed to work consistently with someone who clearly thought he was beneath him?

He flicked another message off to Cillian.

L: Kills, SOS
    L: this is not a drill
    C: meet me at the gate in five

That was a relief. He needed to vent to his best friend and get some perspective. Cillian's heart was in the right place and he had known Link so well for long enough that it made Link feel more himself even imagining seeing him.

He had a spring in his step as he made his way to the main entrance gate to Fairyland and bounced on the balls of his feet as he waited for Cillian. The park wasn't too busy, the post-holiday lull was as close as Fairyland really got to a low season. The cooler weather kept people away, which was probably why Max and Lennon had chosen this time of year to take some of the characters out of the parks to train up for this new programme.

Cillian's distinctive lope caught Link's eye. He was wearing a Prince Magnificence hoodie, in pale purple, which definitely wasn't something he'd have picked out for himself and was absolutely a gift from his boyfriend Grayson. Link's mouth split into a wide smile and he temporarily forgot his woes.

"Well, if it isn't the Prince Magnificence fanclub!"

Cillian rolled his eyes but he was smiling back. "Laugh it up, fairy boy," he said, his Irish accent turning the last word into a drawl. "You try saying no to Grayson when he really wants something."

"I'm sure I have." Link gave Cillian a quick hug hello, and Cillian returned it with warmth.

"Well, he can't have used the puppy dog eyes on you then," Cillian said, sighing. "They're horribly powerful."

"I can imagine." Link plucked at the sleeve of Cillian's hoodie and smiled. "It feels warm at least."

"It's so warm, it's actually really comforting."

"Maybe I should get one, I could use some comfort…" Link sighed. All his troubles came crashing back down on him and he felt his shoulders slump.

"All right, tell me what the problem is, you don't use SOS unless you mean it," Cillian said. He slung a companionable arm around Link's shoulder and led him out of the park.

Link leaned against him without thinking. He and Cillian had always been touchy with each other, but Link had been trying to hold back on that since Cillian started dating Grayson and Haru. But in that moment Cillian's familiar smell of sweat, salt spray from the Pirate's Cove and the lemon ginger kombucha he loved so much was a huge comfort. He leaned in and smelled his best friend and tried not to be creepy about it.

"I have to move," Link said, right before Cillian was about to ask him again. "And I don't want to move, and my new villain is all superior and thinks I'm an idiot."

"Isn't he sort of supposed to be superior and think you're an idiot?"

"Not in real life!" Link pulled away and folded his arms over his chest. "But moving is the real problem. Liam and Roxy just started messaging the group chat with how they're moving out because they have serious relationships and are better than me."

Cillian gave him a sharp look. "Might you be projecting a little of your own insecurities on what they said?"

Link stuck out his tongue but his heart wasn't in it. "Maybe."

"And this happened…?"

"Today, this morning. While I was trying to do all the get to know you and team building stuff with the new guy."

"Well, okay. You need to find a new apartment, it shouldn't be too hard. It'll be a drag but I can keep an eye out and send you anything I think looks promising," Cillian said.

Uh oh, that sounds like he doesn't have time to listen to me whine, Link thought.

"Yeah, I guess so."

"And I'm sure you'll win over your new guy. You were distracted by the moving stuff, you'll feel better once you have a plan."

Link opened his mouth to explain that actually having a plan was kind of the problem, but the bigger problem was money to make that plan happen, but Cillian's phone buzzed and he closed his mouth again.

"Sorry, I just need to check..." Cillian unlocked his phone and an expression of concern flashed over his face. "Ah, okay it looks like Grayson's caught the stomach bug Minako had over the weekend, I kinda have to run and help out."

Link felt his heart sink but he had no interest in being the whiny, needy friend who demanded attention while there were sick kids and boyfriends involved. "Yeah, of course, go take them ginger ale," he said.

"Thanks for understanding." Cillian gave him a quick hug and a kiss on the cheek and then was hurrying off towards his ridiculous vintage car. "I'll talk to you soon!"

Link waved and then turned to his own useless car and drove back to his apartment. If he'd looked out the window and seen a small thundercloud skimming along over his car, he wouldn't have been surprised.

I really hope that it's not like this all day. Or every time we work together.

Lincoln, for some reason, was complaining to Arlo about being paired up with Taeyang for another round of improv exercises.

To be fair, it was only the second day of training and Taeyang had sort of hoped that they'd be given more group work as well. But he'd never dream of making a big deal out of it all the way Lincoln seemed determined to.

"It's on the schedule to do this exercise so that's what we'll be doing," Arlo said. To his credit he was being firm and not wavering even though Lincoln was being sort of bratty. "The point of the exercise is to make the newbies feel comfortable in their roles as villains.

Link folded his arms and pouted, embodying Fairy Mischief as if it were second nature, which… by this point it probably sort of was, Taeyang mused.

"I don't see why we have to make a whole big deal out of the villains," he said.

Ah, so that's the real problem. He doesn't want to share the limelight. Taeyang felt his shoulder muscles tighten with annoyance, he leaned his head side to side to loosen them. *He's so used to being the only one out there with the guests, I suppose. It'd be hard to change your whole modus operandi. But then again, you don't need to make it everyone else's problem. Am I making excuses for him?*

"We are focusing on the villains because that's the theme," Arlo said. "Look Link, please just give it a try, will you? The sooner we have this exercise done the sooner we can break for lunch."

"Fine." Lincoln dropped his hands to his sides and stalked back towards Taeyang. He had been scowling but he had the decency to make his face neutral when he saw Taeyang.

"Right," Arlo raised his voice and everyone went silent. "So we're going to improvise a short scene, try and draw from elements of your movie but make it your own. The premise is you've just surprised each other and you can't fight it out. You have twenty minutes."

Taeyang caught Lincon's eye and smiled encouragingly. "Do you want to start or should I?"

Lincoln shook out his hands and nodded. "You go first, I'll follow."

Taeyang took a quick, focusing breath and cleared his throat, letting his voice ring from his chest as Lord Order's seemed to in the movies.

"Fairy Mischief? You again? What are you doing skulking around my castle?"

Lincoln had half turned away as he'd spoken but now turned back, his eyes wide, as if he'd been caught stealing something. He turned fully to face Taeyang but kept one hand behind his back.

"Me? Skulking? I have no idea what you mean," he said, his voice lighter than normal, more musical almost. It wasn't exactly the same as the voice actor from the movie, but it had the same energy.

Taeyang folded his arms over his chest and looked him up and down, letting all the irritation his character would feel in this moment inform his expression. "What is that you have behind your back?"

Lincoln shifted his weight from one foot to the other and widened his eyes even more. "Behind my back?"

Taeyang took a step closer and drew himself up to his full height, feeling gratified that he was a good five inches taller than Lincoln. "Mischief. You come to my territory, you pretend not to be up to something when it is entirely clear that you are, and now you lie to me?"

He could have kept going. Listing all the ways he was annoyed was quite satisfying, but he paused to give Lincoln time to respond.

"I would never lie," he said, his voice dripping with affronted outrage. "I'm insulted, Lord Order. How dare you speak to me like that!"

Taeyang arched an eyebrow and sneered. "Show me what you have behind your back."

"I won't!" Lincoln took a slight step backwards and Taeyang had a thrill of excitement. Knocking this cocky fairy down a peg was going to be so satisfying.

Taeyang advanced, unfolding his arms with a slow complicated movement he hoped would give him the creepy, spider like mannerisms of the cartoon he was trying to emulate. Lord Order sometimes seemed like he had too many elbows, and it wasn't an easy trick to pull off. Lincoln looked more concerned now, and Taeyang pressed his advantage, looming over him.

"Show it to me or I'll hex your legs again."

"No!" Lincoln had raised his voice again and Taeyang did the same.

"Show me!" he lunged forward as quick as possible, trying to grab Lincoln's arm or snatch whatever he had in his hand. Lincoln snaked away with surprising agility and created a bit more space between them. Taeyang liked the spark in his eye, liked the way he could move his body so smoothly, like a gymnast.

Oh no, he's actually attractive isn't he? I knew objectively he was handsome but he's actually appealing as well. To me. That won't do at all.

"You really want to see it?" Lincoln asked, his voice a little lower and a lot more mischievous. Taeyang could see the signposts to a trap but Lord Order existed to be outsmarted so he went with it.

"Yes, show me. Now."

Lincoln whipped his hand forward and flicked his fingers open as if flinging something in Taeyang's face. "Enjoy your pixie dust!"

Taeyang mimed spitting and scrubbing at his face to rid himself of it. "Disgusting!"

Lincoln laughed and the sound was swallowed up by applause. Taeyang dropped his hands from his face and looked around, surprised. The other character actors were all looking their way and clapping for them. They must have been loud enough to drown everyone out.

He let himself smile a little as Lincoln did the most elaborate and flourish filled bow Taeyang had ever seen. It was utterly ridiculous and endearing at the same time.

"Thank you, thank you, all in a day's work." Then he grabbed Taeyang's hand in his and raised them up in the air as if they were taking a curtain call bow after a show.

Taeyang matched his movement and bowed as he did. "Thanks everyone."

Arlo came forward, his own hands clapping enthusiastically and his clipboard shoved under his armpit. "Brilliant, really great work you two. That's exactly the energy we want to see from all of you."

Taeyang felt flushed with pleasure. Not only had it been genuinely fun to riff off Lincoln in such a way, he was relieved to discover that the disconnected, disaffected behaviour he'd seen from Lincoln didn't mean he was slack at his job. Indeed, now Taeyang was even looking forward to playing against him.

"Thanks," Lincoln said and saluted the room. His eyes seemed to linger on the woman, Rosa, who played Fairy Gentle. Taeyang wondered if there was something going on there, a crush perhaps? Or more likely they were just friends and Lincoln was pleased that she'd seen him perform so well.

"Okay, now you've seen how it's done, please get back to it!"

Arlo turned back to the room. Around the room Lily Ysabel, Stefan and the others turned back to their partners and Taeyang thought he could see renewed determination in their faces. *We've inspired them, we were good enough to inspire them. That's a fantastic thing to learn.*

He faced Lincoln, about to congratulate him on their success but Lincoln was already on his phone, tapping away.

Taeyang felt the happy feeling deflate somewhat and sighed. "I don't think we're supposed to just do one and rest on our laurels," he said. His voice was edged with something annoyingly prissy sounding even to his own ears.

"Yeah," Lincoln said, his eyes still on his phone. "Just gotta..." he spent another twenty seconds tapping at his phone and then pocketed it. "Sorry, back now. Shall I start this time?"

Taeyang cleared his throat and nodded. "Yes, and let's try not to yell this time shall we? Don't want to disrupt the others more than we already have."

I don't know why I said that, I don't know why he's annoying me enough to get snippy with him. I was glad the others liked us a second ago, we were inspiring them. Lincoln's just so irritating.

"THE FACT IS," LINK SAID, LEANING FORWARD TO STEAL ONE OF Cillian's French fries. "He's hot as an underwear model, obviously, which of course he is, they wouldn't have cast him if he wasn't. But it's totally wasted, because he's this control freak who can't loosen up."

Cillian eyed him with something like suspicion. It was Thursday a bit after midday, and they were sitting either side of the small table in the staff room above the Pirate Bay Bar and having their lunches. Cillian's was a large fried tofu combo basket with fries and Link had already finished his sandwich from the Enchanted Forest Kitchen.

It wasn't always easy to make his way through the park to the Pirate Cove to bug Cillian, he wasn't really meant to be seen in other parts of the park in costume and makeup. But he could sneak through the staff only back routes. He'd done that today, after sweet talking Cody to buy him the sandwich and bring it to him so he didn't have to change out of costume for lunch.

The sandwich had been delicious but it wasn't enough food, and Cillian had more fries than he was ever going to eat.

"But you've been out in the park with him now?" Cillian nudged the basket of fries closer to him. Link smiled and helped himself.

"Yeah just on a trial run, though. With him as a minder, you know. Trial stuff while I did my thing." *And he'd looked so cute in the polo and baseball cap...*

"And how'd he do?"

"Yeah, pretty good," Link said. "But...he probably over controlled the crowd. Like there was this one family he hurried off really fast after their photo, there probably could have been more time lingering." He licked the salt off his fingers. "I mean, it was fine. Next week they reckon all the costumes will be ready and then they'll trial us all out together."

"Cool, so have you started looking for a new place?" Cillian asked, with a shade too much nonchalance.

"New place?"

"To live, I assume the flatmates haven't decided not to all move out?"

"You can take the boy out of Ireland, but you can't stop him using British terms apparently," Link said, grinning. He nudged Cillian. "It's roommates here, remember?"

"Right, right." Cillian chuckled and rolled his eyes good naturedly.

Link shook his head and slumped back in his chair. "No, they're all still moving. The place is full of boxes."

"Did you start looking?"

"Yeah, it's fine," Link said, waving his hand. The last thing he needed was Cillian worrying all over him. "There's heaps of stuff around." *I assume. Safest to change the subject.* "How's the love life?"

"Oh you know." Cillian's smile was so warm and gooey Link felt warmth spread through his chest. He really was pleased for his friend. He was glad Cillian had found love. "Busy, but so good." His eyes strayed to his phone.

"I'm happy for you, you deserve it." Link ate a few more fries and sat back in the chair, sighing some. "It's good to see you. We should hang out more. Like, after work sometime soon."

"Yeah for sure," Cillian looked up and smiled. "Just it's a bit busy for the next week or so, but I'll find some time after that, okay?"

"Yeah." Link's smile felt a little more forced than usual. "Of course, whenever works for you."

Soon after, Link made his way back to the Treehouse changing room. He had a good half hour left in his break before he had to get back to whatever training Arlo had planned, and nothing much he had to do before then. He opened up Instagram and started searching for Taeyang.

It didn't take long until he found Taeyang's account, and what he saw there made him wonder if the Fairyland hiring staff had just looked through this and given him the job, no audition required. In between the odd thirst trap of a selfie, the account was entirely photos of a perfectly ordered bookshelf.

Some of the photos showed off the cover of a single book in front of the bookshelf, but it did seem like the real star of the account was the shelf.

It was a very appealing looking bookshelf. There was a photo of every angle imaginable, showing off the books. On each shelf the books were exactly the same height, and the books were ordered by colour - so every shelf had a perfectly uniform rainbow on it.

There were fairy lights in some of the pictures, when Link checked the dates on some of them, they were the festive pictures for Christmas. Fairy lights appeared to be the only way he'd ever decorated the shelves, though, which Link thought was sort of a pity. He could imagine bunches of flowers would look nice, dotted here and there, or candles... although lighting actual fire next to a bunch of books was probably courting disaster. Maybe if you got some of those plastic ones which flickered like candlelight?

He shook his head. He was losing sight of the fact of the anal retentive weirdness of this Instagram account. If you went by this and only this, you'd think his whole life was a bookshelf and whatever book he happened to be reading. Unless...

Link scrolled back through the account and found some other photos, ones where Taeyang seemed to have been experimenting with something called "knolling". Link clicked onto the tag and discovered a whole world of people who took pleasure in carefully arranging things in ordered rows. Cutlery ordered from largest to smallest, each piece just so in perfect lines. He clicked back to Taeyang's feed and found he'd done it with a set of stationery and what must have been the contents of his tool box.

Link laughed out loud, the surprised giggle echoing in the empty room. This man *was* Lord Order. He created order out of his things for fun.

"Absolutely ridiculous," Link said. But he kept scrolling, because there was something deeply satisfying about the pictures. The work that must have gone into them was incredible. And it was pleasing to the eye, everything organized so neatly.

He shook his head and locked his phone. Well, then. Taeyang obviously needed to get laid. Anyone who spent their time creating such carefully arranged social media content was in need of letting loose.

He allowed himself, briefly, to imagine what it might be like to sleep with Taeyang, but then he started to imagine Taeyang trying to lay his lover down just so, and the condom to the side perfectly aligned, the pillow at a perfect right angle to his lover's head and started laughing again.

Much like Lord Order, Taeyang needed to relax. Link could help with that.

8 / TAEYANG

TAEYANG'S PHONE BUZZED AS HE WAS SETTING THINGS UP FOR dinner, and he tapped the screen to accept a video call from his best friend. He propped the phone up on the windowsill so he could keep on chopping vegetables.

"Evening, Min-Jun," he said. He waved at the camera.

"Hello! How's things?" Min-Jun's face appeared, smiling warmly. Taeyang couldn't help but smile back.

"Good, I'm just about to cook dinner though."

"Oooh, what're you having?" Min-Jun craned his neck as if he could lean forward and see what was on the counter. "That's okay, I won't keep you. I just wanted to check in on your new job. It's Thursday on what, your second week? And I haven't had any of the gossip. I figured you'd have been tired out last week but come on."

"Oh, yes, it's good," Taeyang said. "It's well, yes it's going to be a lot of fun, especially going out into the park and meeting people, only…" he trailed off and frowned, not wanting to be rude about Lincoln, but wanting to explain to Min-Jun what the catch was.

"Only?" Min-jun prompted.

"My partner, the one I'm playing opposite," Taeyang said.

"He's very handsome, isn't he?" Min-Jun said. "I've seen him on Instagram and on one of those listicles about the men who

34

work at Fairyland. They called him *the Dreamy Fairy everyone wants to play with*."

"I, yes, but that wasn't what I was going to say," Taeyang said. He pulled out a frying pan and placed it on the element before turning it on. "He just doesn't seem very committed to the role."

"That's a surprise, his pictures make it seem like he's very invested."

"I don't know, the others seem like they're getting on, becoming friends, but every time we're not in an exercise with each other, or given a piece of work to collaborate on, he's on his phone, totally disengaged."

Min-Jun frowned a little. "Maybe he just takes a little time to warm up to people?"

"Maybe." Taeyang sighed. "Or maybe I should make more of an effort."

"I think you should. This is a dream job, and it could be a good long term money-maker for you. Do what you can to make it as pleasant as possible."

Taeyang sighed and considered. Min-Jun was making a lot of sense. Just because he'd had a poor first impression of Lincoln didn't mean he had to keep being wary of him, did it? No, he could make an effort to connect and they'd both be better off for it.

"Yeah, you're right," Taeyang said. He looked at the mountain of vegetables he'd chopped and the oversized portion of chicken he had ready for the fried rice. "Uh, have you eaten? I think I'll have enough to share if you want to come over."

"I'll be right down," Min-Jun said, with no trace of surprise, and hung up the call.

I think he called deliberately at this time because he knew I'd be making dinner, Taeyang thought, amused.

Min-Jun lived in the same building, just a few floors up so they often spent time together. In fact when Min-Jun had first been looking at moving into the building, Taeyang had suggested that he move into Taeyang's spare room, since Taeyang didn't use it for much aside from storing his off-season clothes and his elliptical training machine. Both of which could be moved if Min-Jun wanted the room.

Taeyang left the kitchen to unlock his door and then went back to preparing dinner. His best friend felt more like an annoying younger brother some of the time, but Taeyang liked knowing that he was eating well, so it all worked out nicely.

He let his thoughts stray back to Lincoln, and his undeniably handsome face. He needed to get past the distraction, past the Fairy Mischief act to the person underneath. It might not be easy, but in Taeyang's experience, anything worth having required at least a little work.

9 / LINK

Friday's training was going fine. In fact, Link had an opportunity to skip out on some of it and go out into the park on his own like he always used to do. They'd been doing more improvisation games in pairs for the morning, and then Arlo had announced that the new players, the villains, could all go to Wardrobe for costume fittings.

"Just go through there, that will likely take up the rest of the afternoon. If things are looking good we'll take some makeup test shots, costume poses and so on. So, those of you left, if you'd like to head out for some afternoon Meet and Greets or an encounter or two, go ahead. Just let security know what you're planning so you can have accompaniment."

Link had jumped at the opportunity.

He'd hurried to the Treehouse, practically tore his workout gear off and pulled on the Fairy Mischief shorts and shirt. It was so comfortable, like slipping into pajamas. Not that his workout gear was uncomfortable, but this was better. He had come to realize that being Fairy Mischief was part of who Link was.

His phone had been buzzing with messages from the apartment text and every time it buzzed, Link felt a surge of guilt that he wasn't being more active looking for a new place.

It wasn't a problem that would solve itself, he knew that. But it was just too much to handle. The thought of looking around filled him with dread. He remembered his miserable first few weeks in LA, looking at rat infested basements, lofts with no air conditioning and full afternoon sun, or worse, two room apartments which were absolutely perfect but had already gone to someone else when Link called to say he wanted it.

It was too much. He needed to blow off the bad feelings and the best way to do that was to make some kids laugh.

He did his makeup at lightning speed, not too hard since it mostly consisted of smoky eyeliner and lots of gold glitter.

Getting out into the park was exactly what he'd needed. The bad feelings vanished with every laugh he got to share, and every kid exclaiming "Fairy Mischief!"

"We've missed you," a small blonde girl said. He looked up to see a burly man with a sleeve of tattoos and a leather vest on. He had two more blonde daughters holding each of his hands. Link recognized them from previous visits. They were annual pass holders for Fairyland and Link saw them fairly often.

"Oh, you have?" Link was surprised. It wasn't like he went out into the park every single day even when he wasn't bogged down with training. He went to one knee to be at the eldest daughter's level, what was her name again? Jemima. "I've missed you too, Jemima,. And you, Navi and Stella."

"Yeah, Navi wanted to show you how she can twirl," Jemima said. She turned back to her dad and sisters. "Come on Navi!"

Navi looked up at her father and he nodded. "Go on, he's watching."

Navi dropped her father's hand and took a few steps towards Link. He lived for this stuff. "Go on, Navi, we can twirl together if you like?"

She took a deep breath, raised both arms over her head and spun in a lopsided circle. Link clapped. "That's really impressive!"

Navi grinned and twirled again, so Link jumped up and twirled as well, then he held out his hand to Navi and she twirled while holding his hand. Then the other girls wanted a turn as well, and soon they were all laughing and panting.

"Do dad, too!" Stella, the middle child called out. Link offered his hand to their big biker dad.

"I'm game if you are," Link said, giving him his most winning smile.

The man took his hand gamely and tried to twirl under Link's arm, but Link was a bit shorter and it didn't quite work. Which was great, because it gave everyone more things to laugh about. Then he spun Link around and that went a lot smoother.

"I'm Freddie by the way," the man said. "It's lovely to properly meet you Fairy Mischief, and dance with you."

Link bowed and laughed. "I'd love to dance with you again Freddie, any time you like."

"But, where have you been Mischief?" Jemima asked. "You weren't around any of the days we visited last week."

"And we made dad bring us every day after school," Stella added. Link's gaze flickered to Freddie's face to see if there was any trace of annoyance but he was just smiling. Link got the feeling Freddie would indulge these girls in anything they asked for.

"Well the thing is," Link said. And he lowered his voice to a stage whisper and crouched down, gesturing for them to huddle up. Once they had he continued. "There's rumors that Lord Order is coming to the forest."

Their eyes widened. Jemima took Navi's hand. "Is that so?"

"Well, it's just rumors, right now," Link said. "But I can't risk it so I'm just being kinda careful right now. I had to go check the borders of the forest, and there's this big meetup with the other fairies I have to go to tomorrow." Link bit his lip like he was nervous and then grinned as wide as he could. "I'm sure it'll all be fine."

"You can handle it, Mischief, whatever happens," Stella said, with a determined confidence that Link envied.

That night Link couldn't sleep.

He couldn't sleep and it was Friday night and he hadn't even done anything fun for Friday night, he'd just moped around while Roxy finished packing up her room. Liam was also in the process of moving even though they had another week on the lease, and Link's prospects were bleak.

He'd wanted to have a big apartment dinner together, maybe make a giant bowl of pasta or something and they could all sit around the table and eat and laugh like it was old times. But Roxy was in a hurry.

"I just want to be in the new place already, you know, Linkie?" She'd kissed his cheek with a sad smile when he'd mooted the idea of the dinner. "But we'll definitely have you over for dinner once I'm all settled in, okay?"

Then she'd picked up the packing tape gun and sealed another box and Link had ordered pizza with double cheese and hid in his room, out of the way of the hustle of everyone else moving around and moving out.

ON FRIDAY, TAEYANG AND THE OTHERS WERE SENT INTO WARDROBE
for their costume fitting.

Teddy and Molly, who were the managers of Wardrobe and
seemed to be the most experienced and hands on managers
Taeyang could imagine, had been a delight to work with.

And the costumes were truly divine. Taeyang couldn't help
but feel a thrill of excitement when he was handed his. It was a
coat, fitted over the shoulders and chest and flared out at the
waist, over black slacks with tight interlocking lines forming a
kind of chain or diamond pattern embroidered up the side of
each leg.

"Gorgeous, isn't he?" Molly said, eyeing the coat as Taeyang
held it up to the light. The fabric was a fine satin finish cotton,
heavy but felt breathable. It was gunmetal grey with a fine silver
pinstripe picked through.

The grey, and all the black, would look very striking against
the casual patchwork shorts and shirt Mischief wore, and silver
against Mischief's gold, too.

"Really beautiful," Taeyang said. He ran a finger down one of
the stripes. "I like the contrast you've created against the Mischief
costume, and the way you've heightened the design from the
movie."

"Well, keep talking like that and you'll be my new favorite," Molly said, and gave him a wink. Taeyang laughed. "Now go try it on. We figured the high collar will hide an undershirt so you can just put it on over your T-shirt. I want to check the fit over your hips and your chest."

The fit was almost perfect as it was. He'd given his measurements when he was hired, of course, but there was always a difference between numbers and reality.

He stalked out in the coat, pants, and bare feet and smiled when he heard Lily Ysabel call out.

"Holy crap Lord Order in the house!" She cheered and clapped and some of the others joined in.

"Looking good!" Phoenix James shouted.

Taeyang found he was walking more upright. Something about the way the suit fit across his shoulders made his spine want to straighten, and the flare of the coat from his hips almost to the ground made his walk more dramatic by itself.

"Get out of my way or suffer the consequences!" Taeyang declared, one of Order's lines from the movie.

"You'll have Link kneeling for you in no time," Teddy said, pointing to a little platform. Taeyang stepped onto it. Taeyang instantly pictured Link on his knees and tripped his way onto the platform.

Taeyang wasn't sure that Teddy had meant that in a salacious way but his mind had shorted out at the idea of it.

"I uh, I don't think that's quite the aim," he said.

"Well, you'd be surprised," Molly said. She was already gathering the waist of his coat and pinning it. "I'm starting to think there's a love spell over this whole park."

"A love spell?" Lily Ysabel, who was partially dressed in a form fitting unitard with flowing rags of blue and green asked. She reached out and stroked Taeyang's sleeve. "This is so gorgeous, you could just wear this to a club or something."

"This is not to be worn at a club!" Teddy responded, his hand clutching his chest in horror.

"Yes, a love spell, all the employees keep falling in love with each other," Molly continued. She gestured at Teddy. "Teddy was the last one struck with it, he can tell you while he finishes fitting your skirts."

"Oh, right, yes, sorry." Teddy hustled Lily Ysabel away and got back to work with her costume.

Teddy was dating the man playing Prince Diligence. Taeyang had discovered this when Diligence strode into Wardrobe in full costume, grabbed Teddy and dipped him backwards for a Hollywood style romantic kiss. The others in Wardrobe hooted and applauded and Taeyang did as well, because not only was it brilliantly dramatic, it was rather impressive of the prince to be strong enough to do that with the taller man.

"This is Art," Teddy had said, breathlessly, when he recovered. "I'm sure some of you will end up working with him at some point."

Art waved a hand graciously at them all. "I'm sure I will, especially whoever was lucky enough to be cast as Wizard Haste."

"Oh, that's me!" Stefan raised his hand. "Hi, I'm Stefan." He was being helped into a flowing midnight blue robe with a pattern of lighting forks over the sleeves and around the hem.

"Great to meet you," Art said. He turned to kiss Teddy again. "I'll leave you to it, see you tonight."

Teddy flushed pink and smiled and waved him off. "Yeah, get out of here you boring old hero, we have villains to make fabulous right now."

The costumes really did all look fabulous. Taeyang was reluctant to take his off and the photos they'd taken (against the plainest concrete wall they could find in Wardrobe) all looked incredible.

Taeyang had been so energized and inspired by how he looked in it, he invited the other three around to his house to watch Fairyland movies and have some food over the weekend.

. . .

Stefan, Lily Ysabel and Phoenix James all arrived around noon on Saturday.

"Oh my God, your place is so adorable," Phoenix James said, looking around. "I am obsessed with this bookcase. Like, for real."

"Thanks, it's kinda... I keep it nice for my Instagram," Taeyang said. He didn't have people around much, unless you counted Min-Jun and Taeyang didn't really. Min-Jun was family.

"Oh, are you on Bookstagram?" Lily Ysabel asked. She was trailing a finger over the spines of the books and reading them.

"Yeah, and uh, couple of other platforms too, but Instagram primarily," Taeyang said.

"Wine anyone? It's an Australian Sauv Blanc." Phoenix James was already in the kitchen, pulling open cupboard doors. "As soon as I find the glasses..."

"Yes please!" Lily Ysabel trilled.

"Left cupboard, beside the fridge." Taeyang hurried into the kitchen and helped Phoenix James with getting the glasses out and pouring.

Lily Ysabel and Stefan wandered into the kitchen a little slower, both of them looking around as they did.

"I sort of feel like this is some kind of secret villains cabal," Stefan said as he accepted a glass. "Maybe we ought to have invited the pirates from Pirate's Cove as well?"

"Maybe next time," Lily Ysabel said. "For now I like that it's just us newbies." She took a glass of wine and raised it up.

"What are we toasting?" Phoenix James asked.

"The newbie secret villain cabal, of course." Lily Ysabel laughed and they all clinked their glasses together and echoed the toast.

"That's a nice wine," Taeyang said. "Thanks, Phoenix."

"Phoenix James."

"Phoenix James," Taeyang repeated. "Thanks for the wine."

"It's my pleasure," they said. "So, how's everyone like their partners? And no being nice just for the sake of it. What is exchanged between these walls is kept between these walls. Newbie villain cabal rules."

The afternoon passed in a flurry of gossip and movie watching, and Taeyang relaxed utterly into it. It was good to make new friends, and these people, his coworkers, had quickly become friends.

Link had spent the weekend alternating cleaning his room, checking online listings for apartments, and playing video games. Oh, and not sleeping. Like, hardly at all.

It was all too hard. The apartments which looked alright were few and far between, and without exception when he'd called to enquire, they were already gone. It was disheartening work, hence he'd retreated into his game.

A few hours of gaming later he'd get tired, and go to bed, only to lie there with his eyes open and his thoughts racing a million miles an hour until he gave up and went back to his video game. Sitting in his gaming chair and holding a controller he'd play until his eyes started drooping, then move to bed and stared at the ceiling, wide awake again.

Monday was a refreshing change of pace. It was Taeyang's first outing as Lord Order and they had two Meet and Greets scheduled.

He felt on top of his game as Fairy Mischief. The only problem was the Meet and Greets were the kind that the Princes and Princesses did, with security and a place to stand and Link wasn't supposed to run around and climb trees or play twirling with them. He had to stay put and interact with Taeyang like he was his villain.

The reason for the structure was clear, though. Max had described the week as a kind of 'soft launch' to get the fans excited before they started advertising the 'Season of Villains' properly in a week.

Once the advertising started there would be shows and a new parade, but for this week it was a busy schedule of meet and greets with the other paired up villains and heroes.

After their final appearance for the day, Taeyang and Link were in the changing room together. Taeyang sat at a mirror, removing his makeup carefully with some kind of special makeup removal water. Link usually just used baby oil or a wipe, so he was half watching with a confused fascination.

"I think that went exceptionally well, don't you?" Taeyang asked. He'd possibly noticed Link staring, so Link looked away but then it was weird to be talking to Taeyang and not facing him so he turned back.

"Yeah, it went pretty well," he said. "I mean, yeah it went really well, everyone was lovely and you did great for your first day out there. It's just I'm not so used to those structured meet and greets, so it was a little different for me."

"I suppose it must have been," Taeyang said. "I guess the show and the parade will be even worse for that?"

"Yeah," Link said. "I'm not used to having a set script. I mean, it's fine, like, it's whatever, what we need to do and I get that." He didn't keep going because it was very quickly going to sound like he was complaining about Taeyang being hired and having to work with him, and that was just plain rude.

He didn't want to be rude to Taeyang, well, out of character anyway. In character he could be as rude as he liked.

"I can imagine it would be quite an adjustment, Lincoln."

"It's fine, I'll be fine," Link said. He was feeling sort of weird about Taeyang being so kind and considerate and he wasn't exactly what the feeling was, beyond 'weird'. He could probably tell Taeyang to stop calling him Lincoln and use his nickname like everyone else did, but that felt weird as well. "Uh, don't worry about me or anything."

"Let me know if there's anything I can do to make things a little easier for you." Taeyang set his makeup remover down and ran his hands through his hair, it was carefully sculpted into a villainous sweep in the front, and full of product, but Taeyang managed to muss it enough to look like a hairstyle a normal person might wear. If they were a K-Pop idol, maybe.

What could he possibly do to make things easier for me? I dunno, quit so things could go back to the way they were?

I can't believe I'm resisting change, I'm Fairy Mischief for Pete's sake. I'm meant to embrace the chaos and let Lord Order complain about things changing.

"Yeah, I'll let you know." Link turned back to the mirror and removed his makeup, irritated that it seemed to take much longer than Taeyang's had to remove. His phone buzzed and he picked it up.

"See you tomorrow, Lincoln," Taeyang said.

Link didn't look over from his phone, there was a message from the apartment chat, something about the final clean up at the end of the next week. Link barely registered Taeyang leaving as a wave of doom rolled over him.

"Call me Link," he said, belatedly. But the door to the Treehouse had already closed behind Taeyang.

ON WEDNESDAY TAEYANG WAS FEELING PRETTY CONFIDENT IN himself. The meet and greets with Lincoln had been going very well and he was pleased with the chemistry they had together out in the park. Once they were back in the staff only zones, Lincoln invariably disappeared into this phone and spoke in single syllables but that was all right. Taeyang didn't mind some quiet time to reflect on how things had gone and review his own performance.

He had a notebook he'd been jotting down ideas and thoughts in, so he pulled it out, rested it on his knee and started writing down his thoughts on how the day had gone so far.

There was no denying it, Taeyang was absolutely loving playing Lord Order. The role was hammy, for sure, but the park guests bought into it. He thought back over the people he'd met and settled on one family in particular.

The parents were quiet, their clothes plain and practical. Their child was clutching a Treasure the Unicorn stuffed animal as if her life depended on it. When they got to the front of the queue, Taeyang noticed how all three of them looked a little nervous.

"Go on, it's your turn now," the mother said, and nudged the little girl gently. The girl pressed back against her a little, her eyes wide.

Lincoln was still saying goodbye to the last group, and taking endless selfies with a teenager. It wasn't really Taeyang's place as the villain to invite people forward or to greet people with a friendly smile, but he could draw Lincoln's attention perhaps? Or he could talk to the parents, maybe that wouldn't be too scary for the little girl?

He cleared his throat and raised his hand. "As is right and good, the next person in the queue should step forward, for that is the order of things. Ma'am? Sir? I expect you're here to meet myself, Lord Order. Unfortunately the pest, Fairy Mischief is also here."

That got everyone's attention beautifully. The father laughed a little, sounding less nervous, and moved forward. "Come on Amalie, we can't keep Lord Order waiting now, can we." He bowed to Taeyang.

Lincoln had, of course, been summoned by his name and he stood with his arms folded and his hip popped, shaking his head. "You *really* don't have to bow to this guy, you know."

"Oh, he chooses to bow because he respects me," Taeyang said. "Unlike some fairies I could name."

"Of course," the man said. The little girl and her mother came forward, the little girl was looking between Taeyang and Lincoln with eyes still wide but more full of wonder and amusement than fear.

Lincoln made a raspberry noise and crouched down, smiling at the little girl. "Is your name Amalie? I like your Treasure."

She nodded and held her toy out to Lincoln as if she wanted him to look at it more closely.

Her mother sidled around closer to Taeyang. "You've actually always been my favorite villain," she said. "I've been hoping and hoping to meet you in the park."

Taeyang smiled, genuinely, and then quickly schooled his face to be a little more sinister. "How kind of you to say, Miss...?"

"I'm Rachel, and this is my husband, Sam," she said. "And our daughter, Amalie." She lowered her voice. "We're really hoping things like this will get her out of her shell a little bit."

Taeyang nodded once, his mind racing. He wanted to make

this a good experience for Amalie, he knew all too well what it was like to be a shy and introverted child. "Fairy Mischief leave the child alone," he said.

Lincoln looked up, perhaps startled. "What? She's showing me her Treasure plush."

"She's obviously here to visit me, kindly let her by so she can bask in my greatness."

Amalie looked at Lincoln and then up at Taeyang. She stuffed her unicorn plush under one arm and side-stepped Lincoln to approach Taeyang. "Hello, Mister Order," she said. Her voice was quiet but had certainty to it.

"Hello," Taeyang said. "Of course it's a pleasure to see you here in my forest."

"My forest," Lincoln said. He got to his feet and pouted.

Amalie reached for Taeyang's hand and looked to her mother. "Can you take a photo, please, Mom?"

"Of course!" Rachel fumbled in her pocket and produced a phone. Lincoln moved behind them, and Taeyang assumed it was to photobomb after the first few shots were taken. He imagined Lincoln was pulling some truly hideous faces, so he posed seriously for a few more photos then pretended to notice what Lincoln was doing.

"How dare you!" Taeyang said. Sam and Rachel immediately burst into laughter as Taeyang turned to Lincoln. "You are interrupting my very important meeting with Amalie."

"It's all right," Amalie said, giggling as well. "He can be in the picture, too."

"Thank you, Amalie," Lincoln said. He moved to stand directly in front of Taeyang.

Taeyang suppressed the urge to kick him out of the way and instead cleared his throat extremely loudly. "Perhaps you could stand on the other side of Amalie?"

"I like it here."

The family had giggled all through the process, and when they'd finally moved away, Amalie had waved and blown a kiss at Taeyang, not at Lincoln.

In the two seconds they had before the next family came up, Lincoln had whispered. "Great work" to Taeyang.

Those two words had made Taeyang prouder and more pleased than he'd expected they would. They assured him that his gut was right, and he was doing well. Lincoln might be annoying and somewhat disconnected when they weren't in the park facing customers, but he was good out there. He knew what he was doing, and the fact he'd recognized Taeyang's work was encouraging.

Later on, when they were back in the Treehouse on break, he considered getting Lincoln's attention and asking to talk through in more detail what had worked and what hadn't, but when he looked over again, Lincoln had put in headphones and was staring so intensely at his phone Taeyang assumed he was watching a TV show.

The door to the tree changing room banged open and Phoenix James and Rosa came in, both of them laughing. Rosa was clutching at Phoenix James's arm.

"I can't believe you actually went there!" Rosa laughed.

Taeyang set his notebook down and grinned at the two of them. "Had a good time out there?"

Phoenix James looked over at Taeyang and nodded, their eyes wide. "I don't think I've ever had so much fun at a job before, in my whole life. And I used to work as an exhibition skater at a roller disco!"

Rosa burst into giggles. "Of course you did!"

"That must have been a lot of fun," Taeyang said. Phoenix James preened and brushed an imaginary piece of lint off their shoulder.

"It was hard work, don't get me wrong, but it's pretty hard not to be happy while people are looking at you with such admiration and envy. Besides it's kinda impossible to not feel up while listening to ABBA don't you think?"

"You're probably right." Taeyang grinned as Phoenix James flopped down in the chair beside him.

"It's hot out there though, I thought this was low season

because it's not as warm." Phoenix James picked up a villains flyer and fanned themself with it.

"It is hot," Taeyang said. He'd unbuttoned and removed his long coat the instant he was inside and was finding it a bit warm in the treehouse even with just his T-shirt.

"I'll turn up the air conditioning, it's just over here, newbies, for reference." Rosa went to the wall and tapped the controller.

She glanced at Lincoln who had barely looked up since they came in. Her expression got a bit more serious and she flitted back over to lean towards Taeyang. "Is he all right?"

Taeyang followed her gaze towards Lincoln and shrugged. "I really wouldn't know, this is how he seems to act."

"It's not... entirely normal for him," Rosa said. "I'll check in." She walked towards Lincoln, who looked up as she approached and pulled out his earphones, giving her a friendly smile that Taeyang felt a little jealous he'd never been on the receiving end of.

13 / LINK

ROSA'S WORDS STUCK IN LINK'S HEAD. HE DIDN'T LIKE THAT SHE'D noticed he was stuck in his phone and not really... interacting with the others.

"It's not like you, you're usually the life of the party," Rosa had said. She reached for his hand, which Link wasn't totally happy about, because he was using his hand to scan online listings for apartments, of which there were none. But aside from that, he and Rosa had never exactly been close. He'd had a rivalry going with her inside his head, ever since she'd made Fairy Gentle so wildly popular with her portrayal.

"Yeah, I'm just, uh, dealing with some life stuff at the moment," Link said. "Thanks for... checking in? I guess?" He hoped she'd get the hint so he could try another platform but she leaned forward.

"It's just that the rest of us have really been enjoying the new stuff, you know, working alongside a villain. If it's not working out for you, you can always talk to Arlo, or to me." She gave him an encouraging smile. "Because we're all here to support you."

Link bit his tongue so he didn't ask her to find him an apartment or something similar. He didn't want to be the guy who complained about moving house, and he didn't want her sympathy. Heinhaled and shook his head.

"It's not that, Taeyang is fine, it's fine, although admittedly it's been a bit of an adjustment, but it's fine. I just need to sort this out." He shook his phone to show her he needed time alone with it. "Then it'll be fine."

How many times did I just say the word fine? Surely she'll get the hint and back off, please universe, if you've ever loved me.

"Okay," Rosa patted his arm. "Just let me know if there's anything I can do to help, okay?"

"Yeah, thanks," Link said. He gave her a smile he knew was more of a grimace and then started scrolling again.

Thursday's schedule was for a meet and greet in the morning and then some more training with Arlo in the afternoon with the other pairs of heroes and villains. It shouldn't be too hard a day, which was good news because Link had spent much of the night staring at his bedroom ceiling or scrolling through Taeyang's Instagram to try and put himself to sleep.

Link's car made a disturbing noise when he went to start it up, so he turned the ignition off, counted to ten and tried again. This time it started normally and he gave it a severe talking to. "None of that, thanks very much. I have enough on my mind right now without you giving up."

The car took him to work just fine, but the weird noise had unsettled him. Inside the park he made his way straight to the Treehouse. He wanted a coffee, even was tantalized by the scent of it wafting by when he walked past the Enchanted Forest Kitchen, but his funds were getting low, and he needed to save for the move, especially if he needed to make a security deposit on a new place. It felt far too late to try and find new roommates now, and he'd just kind of blanked on it even being a possibility anyway. Too hard basket, so now he was thinking about money instead.

He groaned to himself, remembering that a security deposit would probably be a full month's rent, plus security deposit plus the previous month's rent... it would be a big chunk, and he had no savings to speak of. He'd better not spend anything at all if he could help it.

Taeyang was already inside when Link scanned in, and Rosa was lounging in her dusky pink fairy tunic and shorts combo, drinking something that looked to be coffee under all the whipped cream and syrup.

"Morning all," Link said. Both of them looked over at him, Rosa with a concerned eyebrow crinkle and Taeyang with a strange expression, which could have been annoyance or could have been hopefulness.

"Good morning, Lincoln," Taeyang said. It was a testament to how out of sorts Link felt that he didn't tell him to use his nickname.

"Hey, Link," Rosa said. Then everyone lapsed into silence.

Link took his normal set up place and started on his makeup, using a bit of extra concealer under his eyes to hide the darkening bags there.

Can't be Fairy Mischief who looks like he's never slept. Have to look cute and young and full of energy. A coffee would have really helped...

Things perked up when Phoenix James arrived. Phoenix James always had the energy to light up the room and get them all laughing. Link felt a bit better as they set out into the park proper at the same time.

"We're not doing all four of you together at once," Arlo said, when he came to fetch them with their security detail. "Not just yet. Link, Taeyang, you'll be by the reflecting lake and Rosa and Phoenix James you can have the rose arbor again, since it worked so well for you yesterday."

"Awesome, thanks Arlo," Rosa said.

The morning went irritatingly well by the reflecting pool. There was really no reason to be annoyed that Taeyang was good at his job, but Link was feeling it anyway. He had the posture down, the mannerisms, the intonation of this voice as he spoke. It was like the cartoon character had come to life and was making fun of Link at every opportunity.

And, even worse, Link couldn't even be sullen about it. He

had to be upbeat as Fairy Mischief, he had to be fun personified, and for perhaps the first time Link could remember, that wasn't coming easily to him.

He was so tired, his head was aching and there was a kind of thumping behind his left eyeball that he was finding it hard to ignore. He gritted his teeth and tried to put Link out of his mind. There was no Link, there was only Fairy Mischief, and he had a Lord Order right there to trick and visitors he needed to make laugh.

After a while it had started to work, and especially when he was doing silly things like tweaking the skirt of Taeyang's coat, or pulling faces for photos of Lord Order, things became easier. By the time they were heading back to the Treehouse, Link felt more on top of things. He was still tired out, for sure, but he wasn't feeling as doom and gloom as he had that morning. It was still irritating how effortless Taeyang made it all seem.

It's as if he never has a bad day, I wonder what his secret is. Maybe it's just because he's so new to it all, and I'm getting jaded. I hope not...

They changed out of their costumes, and wiped off their makeup.

Taeyang cleared his throat and approached Link, his soft grey T-shirt was accentuating a dancer's body, all muscles and pleasant angles. Link tried not to notice.

"Lincoln, I was wondering if you might like to get lunch with me?" He asked.

Link had no reason to say no, none at all. But he was in a mood still, and he didn't want to spend the next hour staring into Taeyang's perfect face while he ate the cheapest thing available.

"Oh, uh, thanks but I actually have plans," Link said. "Across the park with my best friend, he works as a pirate in Pirate Bay."

He had no such plans and for a moment it looked as if Taeyang was going to question him about it, but he shook his head slightly. "Maybe tomorrow then? I feel like we need some time to properly talk with each other, clear the air."

Urgh, now I feel guilty, he's right, we do need to actually talk. But I'm too tired, I just can't face it today.

"Yeah, tomorrow, that sounds great." Link gave a half-hearted thumbs up and then cringed at himself.

Taeyang raised his eyebrows and nodded. "Tomorrow it is, then." And he left Link alone.

What the hell was that?

"THANKS FOR GETTING HERE SO PROMPTLY AFTER LUNCH," ARLO
said. Once again they were back in the dance practice room for
training. There were three rows of folding chairs, which once
again felt like far too many for the group attending. Arlo stood up
front of the chairs with a table laden with craft supplies. Taeyang
wasn't sure what to expect, but he was hopeful. Arlo's exercises
had all been interesting so far.

"I know you've all been doing well on your adventures out
into the park. So you should all congratulate yourselves on that."

There was a soft murmur from the others, Rosa patted Phoenix
James on the shoulder and Stefan chuckled. "Yes, I am the best!"

Taeyang looked around for Lincoln to give him a smile but
Lincoln was in a seat in the row behind, buried in a hoodie too big
for him and staring into the middle distance.

*I can't tell if there's something really bothering him or if he's just
totally disengaged from this whole programme. Rosa did say he wasn't
acting like himself.*

I really hope it's not because he has to work with me.

"Right, so this activity is for all of you to appreciate each
other," Arlo said. "I know this is going to sound a little cheesy, but
bear with me, okay? First, come up and grab one of these big
pieces of paper, a marker and some sticky notes."

Lily Ysabel was in the front row, so she was the first to the table. She picked up the stack of papers and took one, then passed the stack to Taeyang. He took one and passed it to Rosa. Meanwhile Lily Ysabel was handing out pens and sticky notes. Arlo smiled, watching them.

"Bet you were always the one sticking your hand up in class and doing all the work in group projects," Lincoln said when Lily Ysabel gave him a pen and some notes. She smiled and gave him a wink.

"I might have been."

"Okay, so on the big piece of paper, I want you to draw a bucket," Arlo said. "Like, a big bucket, make it take up most of the page."

"A bucket?" Phoenix James asked. "Why?"

"It will become obvious shortly," Arlo said. "Here's one I already did." He held up a piece of paper with a large outline of a bucket shape on it.

Taeyang tried his best to copy it, making sure his bucket outline was as symmetrical as he could make it. It didn't look too bad.

"Has everyone got a bucket?" Arlo looked around the room, and Taeyang's eyes strayed to Lincoln again. He was drawing a bucket that didn't fill the page and was clearly lopsided.

"Yeah," Stefan said.

"Great, now write your name in it. Your real name, not your character name, just in case that wasn't clear. Maybe just at the top or at the bottom. Not right in the middle, anyway."

Taeyang wrote "Tae" at the top of his bucket. Not that anyone in the park actually used a nickname for him, but maybe they would if they saw it was an option?

"Okay, thanks. Now, take some of this tape and stick your bucket poster up on the wall, anywhere in the room."

It took about five minutes, everyone grabbing tape and choosing a spot on the wall. Taeyang put his right next to Lily Ysabel's, because she'd drawn a very nice looking bucket. The others put theirs scattered about the room, at least one on each of the four walls.

Stefan laughingly pretended to stick his up over Nate's. Nate shoved him playfully in the ribs and they had a friendly tussle.

"Okay, everyone got a bucket with their name on up on the wall? Yes?"

"Yes," Taeyang said.

"Right, the next part is the fun bit. The idea here is that everyone has a bucket, and you can fill each other's buckets by putting nice words into it. So, a compliment makes the person receiving it feel good right? That's filling up their bucket, and the best thing is, doing that for someone else fills your bucket too."

There was a moment while everyone looked at each other in disbelief.

"Is uh, is this an activity they do in kindergarten?" Julia asked. Taeyang hadn't spoken to Julia much but she seemed to match Lincoln for her level of skepticism.

"Uh, well, sort of," Arlo said. His cheeks flushed and he looked at the ceiling for a moment before continuing. "It did start as a picture book I think, but it works really well for adults too. I don't think adults compliment each other enough, and this is an easy way to do that and to see that others appreciate you. Would you give it a try? I know it might seem cheesy, but just try."

"Hey, we work at Fairyland, we can do cheesy," Nate said. Everyone chuckled and Taeyang liked Nate a bit more, the way he'd put them all at ease was effortless and kind.

"Right, so go for it," Arlo said. "I won't time you, just write as many as you can and then come sit down when you're done."

Taeyang's bucket was right beside Lily Ysabel's, so he wrote a sticky note for her first. 'Flawless queen' and stuck it up. She was writing something for his bucket too, but he decided not to look until the end. Instead he made his way around the room, finding a nice thing to say about each of them, and especially taking some time with Nate's one to say he admired the way he could put people at ease.

The last bucket he reached was Lincoln's, and he'd put 'Link' up the top, a nickname that Taeyang had seldom felt he could use for him. By all rights this should be the easiest one to fill out, he'd spent more time with Lincoln than anyone else in the room. But when he put his pen to the sticky note he found his mind blank.

He looked over what everyone else had written, and it was almost entirely 'great sense of humor' related comments. Taeyang had to do better than that.

'Fantastic to work with', he wrote, and stuck it on the bucket. Then, on impulse, he quickly scribbled another one. 'Would like to get to know you better'. Once the words were written, he looked at them doubtfully. Maybe it was too much?

No, I wanted to write it, and this exercise is about getting to know each other, about strengthening bonds. I should let him know.

He stuck the note in Lincoln's bucket and went to sit down. Lincoln was already seated, his phone in his hand and his thumbs flying as if he were typing a very important message to someone.

Rosa was the last to sit down. Arlo clapped his hands. "Good work everyone! I hope that wasn't too hard. Now, the fun bit. Go back to your own bucket and see what nice things people have said about you."

Taeyang went to his bucket and scanned the sticky notes, disappointed when he realized that he didn't know Lincoln's handwriting. He read them one by one and was pleased to find that Arlo was right. It did make him feel good to see the nice things people had written about him.

'A natural at being a villain,', 'great to talk to', 'Handsome af', 'kind' and 'a brilliant Lord Order'.

His eyes returned to the one that said he was handsome. He wondered if it was a joke, something Lily Ysabel had put in there to tease him.

"Okay, who said I was handsome af?" Nate called out across the room, laughing. "You might want to take this back and burn it. Because my boyfriend has a particular set of skills and he will find you and kill you if he finds out you were thinking this."

Lincoln laughed out loud and stuck his hand up. "Guilty! What can I say, I like to cause mischief." Nate balled up the sticky note and tossed it at Lincoln, who slipped a hand behind his back and caught it that way, like a trick baseball player.

"That's funny, I have one that says 'Handsome af' as well," Rosa said. The others laughed, Taeyang looked down at his and nodded once.

All right, it was a joke, he must have just said the same to everyone. Objectively it's a good joke, so why do I feel let down?

"All right, those posters are yours to take home or put up by your changing station or whatever you like," Arlo said. "Thanks for being good sports about it."

"This was a really lovely exercise," Lily Ysabel said. "Thanks Arlo. I think we ought to do it again in a few weeks. I really like seeing how much people appreciate me."

Arlo smiled so wide Taeyang thought his cheeks would ache. "You're welcome. I'm glad you liked it. Okay, for the rest of the afternoon we're just going to go around and share our experiences out in the park, what worked, what maybe didn't work quite so well, so grab your chair and we'll put them in a circle and start the discussion."

THE LUNCH THAT LINK HAD AGREED TO HAVE WITH TAEYANG WAS weighing on his mind, and he didn't know why. What was it about Taeyang that had him feeling so off footed, so not quite right?

He watched him, during their first meet and greet of the day. He was perfect, really. Magnificently handsome and formidable in his Lord Order costume with the impressive coat. It was ironic that Link was finding it irritating that Taeyang made acting look so easy. Link had found Fairy Mischief easy for his entire career. Well, until he'd stopped sleeping because there wasn't a single room available for rent anywhere in LA.

But even sleep-deprived, working with Taeyang made being cheery and cheeky easier. He was a joy to play against, it was just that Link was having a lot of trouble feeling joy right now. He was the last one in his apartment, Liam had moved out the night before and taken the couch from the lounge. All there was left in Link's apartment was Link and his things. It was depressing. And the lease was going to expire and then what?

Taeyang cleared his throat and Link realised he'd been chewing his nails while they waited for the next person in line. *Focus Link, you can't lose this job. Fairy Mischief does not chew his nails so neither can you.*

He spent the next hour being the best possible Fairy Mischief he could manage, laughing a bit too loud and pulling faces and yanking on Taeyang's sleeve so he'd have to adjust the way his coat sat on his shoulders.

When they got back to the Treehouse, he flopped onto the chair in front of his make up station, feeling wrung out.

"If we change and go now, we should beat the lunch rush," Taeyang said. Link startled, having more or less forgotten about the lunch in his exhaustion.

"Yep, just give me a second," Link said. He took a deep breath and tried to think of a good excuse to bail on lunch, but his brain didn't comply with anything useful. And his stomach was rumbling. He had to eat.

He pulled himself to his feet, pulled on some loose sweatpants over his Fairy Mischief shorts, and a Davey Typhoon hoodie over his tunic. He swiped a wet wipe over his face to remove as much of the glitter as he could and shoved his feet into sneakers. "Ready."

Taeyang had changed into a Fairy Mischief T-shirt with a grey hoodie over the top and loose but perfectly fitted jeans. Link found himself grinning at the choice of T-shirt. Maybe it was a peace offering of a sort?

"When did you pick that up?"

Taeyang glanced down at himself, as if he hadn't worn it expecting it to be noticed. But it was obviously a bid for attention of some kind. "Oh this? I just got it at the gift shop the other day, it was on sale."

"Mmhm." Link felt a little like his old self again for a moment, enjoying this moment of possible power over Taeyang. "I bet they had the Fairy Gentle shirts on sale, too. And the Sing and Dance ones too."

Taeyang grinned and looked away. "Well, it felt disloyal to get one of those designs."

"Disloyal?" Link laughed. "That's very sweet of you."

"Let's just go to lunch." Taeyang ducked his head.

"Okay, but for the record, it's a cute gesture, and I appreciate it." Taeyang had already turned away, leading the way to the Enchanted Forest Kitchen.

The harsh sunlight hurt Link's eyes and he wished he'd put on a baseball cap to protect himself. It brought back his tiredness.

Taeyang got them seated at a booth and they were both looking over the menus when Link yawned so wide he almost dislocated his jaw.

"I'm sorry for not being better company," Taeyang said drily. Link was suddenly sorry he hadn't been able to keep up the joking and almost flirty conversation from earlier. But he didn't have the energy. He needed to preserve what little energy he had for the afternoon's meet and greets.

"Sorry, it's not you," he said. He sighed. There was really no reason not to tell Taeyang about his woes, at least a little. Taeyang was being directly affected after all, more than anyone else in Link's life.

Especially since Cillian's been so busy...

"I've just been kind of... well, if I'm honest. I'm totally overwhelmed and I'm not sleeping because of it." Link rubbed his forehead and let his hands fall to his lap. It felt weird to admit he was overwhelmed, uncomfortable.

"Overwhelmed? I'm sorry, is this because of me? The changes to your role?"

Link shook his head. "No, well, to tell the truth, it hasn't helped. But there's other stuff going on, outside of work."

He felt his heart racing in his chest as if he were about to confess something world changing or terribly vulnerable. Like he was going to tell Taeyang he loved him, which was ridiculous, because he clearly didn't.

"You don't have to tell me, if you don't want to," Taeyang said.

A waiter came to their table. His nametag said 'Tim'. "Hey, are you two ready to order?"

Link looked down at his menu, he hadn't read any of it, but he knew what was good at this place. "Uh, yeah the roast and vegetables please." He could splash out on food now and then go without dinner, maybe.

"Same for me," Taeyang said. "And a cola."

"Awesome, any drinks for you, sir?" Tim fixed Link with a look of such bright intensity Link had the irrational urge to slap the notepad out of his hand.

"Uh, yeah, just a lemonade thanks."

Tim repeated their order back and then hurried off with the menus, Link looked at the table and then up at Taeyang.

He wasn't prepared for what he saw in Taeyang's expression and it made his heart skip some. Taeyang was giving him a soft look, all compassion and openness and he so clearly wanted him to open up and explain what was happening it was probably cruel not to.

"I guess the biggest problem is my roommates have all moved out, and I need to find a new place in a week." Link said. "Or I guess I'm living out of my car, which could break down at any moment because it's a piece of junk. And yeah, I've looked at all the online listings and I can't find anything that isn't already gone by the time I call them." He sighed and propped his chin on his hand and his elbow on the table. "And then my job changed."

TAEYANG HADN'T EXPECTED THAT. HE'D EXPECTED LINCOLN TO complain about Taeyang intruding on his gig, on making things harder than they had been, even though appearing together had been not only painless but good fun.

Instead, Lincoln had admitted he was in quite dire straits.

For a beat, Taeyang watched him, as if he was just about to burst out laughing and say it was a joke, but he didn't. He actually looked more like he was about to cry.

Taeyang had to say something. "I had no idea, that sounds awful."

"It straight up sucks," Lincoln said. He pressed both his hands over his face and sighed heavily before propping his chin on his hand again. "So yeah, sorry if I haven't been a hundred percent awesome."

"That's, that should be the least of your worries." Taeyang tapped his fingers on the tabletop. "I've seen online how hard it is to find a place right now. The housing market is just swamped, they say…"

The waiter returned with their drinks. "Your food is just a couple of minutes away," he said, and hurried off again.

Taeyang looked around the Enchanted Forest Kitchen. But he didn't take in any of the things he saw, his mind was racing, trying to find some kind of solution for the sad man sitting opposite him. He couldn't stand the way Lincoln looked. The tug of his mouth going down, it went straight to Taeyang's heart. There had to be something he could do...

He needed a place to stay. Taeyang slapped the table.

"I've got it."

Lincoln startled, he had possibly been falling asleep with his chin on his hand. He folded his hands in his lap and shook his head.

"What have you got?"

"A spare room, it's just got a couple of things in it and I can move them, you can use my spare room. Just until you find something." Taeyang smiled, hoping he was looking encouraging.

Lincoln blinked at him as if he'd just started speaking in Korean. "What the fuck?"

Taeyang shook his head. "It's a good solution, you can move in right away and then you don't have to worry about the lease, or living in your car. You can stay while you find something new, it's basically sitting there empty at the moment."

"I..." Lincoln's face flushed pink and he shook his head. "No, thanks. Taeyang that's too much, I can't do that. Thanks for the offer, but it's... no, I'll find something."

"Think about it at least," Taeyang said. He knew he was pressing Link, but he didn't see any problem with it as a solution. "We could carpool to work, both of us save a bit of money."

Lincoln chewed his lip and it did look like he was considering it. Then Tim reappeared with trays of food and cutlery and set them down in front of them.

"Enjoy!"

Taeyang inhaled the delicious smell of the roast beef and cleared his throat. "Just, think about it, okay? We can talk about something else for now if you'd rather."

"Yeah. Yeah, thanks for the offer," Lincoln said. He speared a piece of beef with his fork and pointed it at Taeyang. "That was very kind of you."

Taeyang shook his head and started to eat. "It's the least I could do."

The two of them ate in silence for a minute or two and then Taeyang figured it was up to him to introduce a new topic so he fell back on his original plan for the lunch. "So, uh, I'm open to feedback on how I've been doing, you know. Out there in the park. If there's any hints you want to give me I'd be happy to hear them."

Lincoln looked up, and Taeyang once again got the feeling his thoughts had been miles away. But at least now he knew what Lincoln was worried about.

"Uh, well, you've actually really been impressing me," he said. "I can't immediately think of anything I could tell you... maybe get down on the kid's level a bit more but then, it actually makes a lot of sense for your character not to. I don't mind if you leave that to me, my costume's built for it and yours... kind of isn't."

"Very true, although I'm sure I'm going to have some children become fans and then I'll have to adjust how I interact," Taeyang said. He hoped Lincoln could tell he was joking.

Lincoln grinned and his eyes flashed, *oh yeah, he can tell.*

"Unlikely," he said. He licked a bit of gravy off his lip and Taeyang was far too distracted by the tongue to immediately respond. "How many kids do you know who enjoy tidying their room? Uh-uh, the kids like you, but they're *fans* of Fairy Mischief. Of me.."

"Well, we'll see..." Taeyang said, letting a little of the timbre of Lord Order's voice go into his words.

17 /LINK

Link was still sort of reeling from how lunch had gone. They'd done their last park appearance for the day, for the week even, and he was cleaning off his makeup when his phone buzzed. Cillian's name flashed up.

Cillian: sorry I've been such a bad friend, treat you to dinner?

Link smiled and texted back, feeling a bit superior and a bit pleased.

Link: well, I don't know. I might be too busy and important

Cillian: don't make me beg, Fairy Boy

Link: fine, I guess I can see you. But heads up I'm totally exhausted so I don't want a late one

Cillian: no worries, meet me at the Intergalactic Diner and we'll catch up

Link grinned at himself in the mirror. He had missed his best friend, and although he was happy for him, finding love and all, he was selfishly annoyed he didn't get to see as much of him as he'd used to.

He stood up and pulled on his Davey Typhoon hoodie. "Catch you later," he said to Taeyang.

"Oh, hey, take my number," Taeyang said. He was half dressed but he set down his shirt and picked up his phone. "Tell me yours and I'll text you, then if you, you know, decide you want my spare room you can get in touch. Because you'll have my number."

Link hadn't expected that. Taeyang's offer at lunch had been sweet and kind and utterly out of the blue. Link hadn't thought he'd really meant it besides trying to offer a solution in the moment. Maybe the offer really was legit?

Link rattled off his phone number and Taeyang added him on a texting app. "Right, cool. Thanks," Link said.

"Seriously, get in touch if you need to," Taeyang said. His eyes met Link's with a ferocious intensity that set something going in Link's chest. It was even more attractive than Taeyang was most of the time, and it gave him a warm feeling through his center. And slightly below as well…

No, can't think about that, that's a very bad idea and I won't… I won't even consider how handsome and intense he is and how much I want him to push me against a wall and kiss me. And how he has no shirt on right now. Nope, none of that.

Link shook his head. "Yeah, thanks. Have a good weekend."

He fled the treehouse and took a deep breath.

None of that was real, I'm just responding like that because I'm tired and because he offered a room. He offered to take care of me.

Link put his head down, pocketed his phone and made his way across the park to the Hidden Galaxy area. He relaxed the further he got from the Enchanted Forest and Taeyang.

Cillian was already seated at a booth in the diner, a purple drink with boba in it sitting in front of him.

"Is that for me?" Link said, flopping down opposite him. "Or have you decided to give up on being a vessel only for healthy food?"

"Oh, it's for you obviously," Cillian said. He pushed the cup towards Link. "My kombucha is taking longer to make than whatever this sugary monstrosity is."

"Thank you, looks incredible." He sipped the drink and made a satisfied noise. "Tastes like purple."

"You are a gigantic child," Cillian said, laughing. "Now, tell me how the apartment hunt is going."

Link tried not to wince at being called a child or the mention of the words apartment hunt, but it was a failure. He knew Cillian was joking, and joking affectionately, but he was so wrung out it just felt mean.

"Awful," he said, looking at the table. "There's nothing. Absolutely nothing, I might have to move back in with my folks."

"Don't they live in San Diego?" Cillian kicked Link gently in the ankle until Link looked up.

"Yeah. The commute would be killer..."

"It's a pity this didn't happen a month from now," Cillian said. "You could just take my lease from me."

"Your lease?" Link tilted his head to the side. "I didn't know you were moving."

"Oh yeah, Haru found a new place and it's big enough for all of us, kid, giant puppy and the dog included." Cillian smiled, clearly over the moon.

"Wait, giant puppy *and* the dog? I thought Grayson just had one dog, you're getting a puppy?"

"Grayson is the giant puppy," Cillian said. His smile was so warm and affectionate it made Link want to punch him. He had everything Link didn't.

"Right, but you can't move in for a month?"

"No, we're getting the bathroom fixed up, it's gonna take that long. I mean you could always sleep on my couch 'til then I guess?" Cillian frowned. He'd offered but Link knew it would be a nightmare if he moved into Cillian's, the apartment was barely big enough for Cillian as it was, and the couch was on the way from the bedroom to the bathroom. They'd be on top of each other at all hours.

"I don't think that would work," Link said. "But thanks."

"Maybe I could stay with Gray, while-"

Link shook his head. "No it's fine, I actually..." He rubbed a hand over his forehead. "Taeyang offered me his spare room."

"He did?" Cillian's expression cleared and he sat back in his seat, suddenly looking more relaxed. "That's great, you two are really getting on well, huh?"

"Yeah, we're getting on okay," Link said. "I mean, I've been out of my head pretty much. So I've not, you know, been as charming as normal, but he's very kind, I guess."

"Well, that's great, you can use his spare room for the next few weeks and then when my new place is ready you can take over the lease on my old one."

Link breathed out and nodded, he could see that working. The timeframes sucked, and having to move twice would be a massive drag, but at least he knew Cillian's place, where it was, how to get around from there. And it was small enough he wouldn't need roommates.

"Okay, yeah that… that might work, huh?" He asked, even though he knew it would. There was a fluttering feeling in his chest, and it needed reassurance.

"Damn right it will work." Cillian grinned and nudged a menu towards Link. "Now decide what you want to eat so we can order, my stomach's rumbling loud enough to wake the kraken."

"Okay yeah, just let me…" Link sent a message to Taeyang accepting his offer of the spare room. "Right, planet shaped nuggets or Mayhem burger?"

"You should get a salad," Cillian said.

"The burger has lettuce in it, that'll do."

18 / TAEYANG

TAEYANG HAD SEEN THE EXPRESSION ON LINCOLN'S FACE, AND HAD taken that as his answer, Lincoln wouldn't accept his offer of a spare room.

So, when he got the text thanking him for offering and said he would take the room, Taeyang didn't know what to do with it.

He drove home, trying to mull on what he was feeling, but came up with nothing but confusion. He went up to Min-Jun's apartment instead of his own and knocked on the door.

Min-Jun opened the door, his face expectant, and his expression fell, seeing Taeyang there.

"I thought you were my pizza."

"Uh, no, I just wanted to talk," Taeyang said. He hadn't even considered dinner, he was so wrapped up in his own thoughts.

"Come in, then, but I'm gonna start eating when my pizza gets here." Min-Jun held the door open and Taeyang went in, leaving his shoes next to Min-Jun's. "What's up? You want a beer?"

"Sure." Taeyang accepted the bottle of beer and they both sat on the couch. Taeyang chewed his lip, not sure where to start. Min-Jun tapped his foot, looking expectant.

"You wanted to talk, you said?"

"Yeah, I'm just trying to work out where to start." He sat back, taking a swig of beer. "I offered my spare room to Lincoln."

"The guy who plays Fairy Mischief is moving into your apartment?"

"Well, he wasn't going to accept I think, but now he has, and he's... yeah, going to move in. Just for a few weeks, his current apartment's lease is running out and he's not been able to find anything else."

"Okay, so what's the problem?" Min-Jun said. "You offered the room, he said yes, you're helping him out. Sounds good."

"I just don't know what I was thinking, I mean I barely know the guy, and he's kinda... you know, a bit hopeless."

Min-Jun smiled then, his expression a bit sly. "Wait, so you acted on impulse? You? You barely know the guy and you offered him your room?" Min-Jun spoke as if he'd worked out a puzzle that Taeyang hadn't yet.

"Yes? And now I'm regretting it. What if he messes up my house?"

"Did you consider that maybe the problem isn't that he'll make a mess, it's that he'll be in close proximity and you're feeling something for him? Something less than professional?" Min-Jun suggested.

Taeyang's hand paused on the way to lifting the beer bottle to his lips. "Uh, no, I just... I work with him, I need him to stick around or my role's kind of... nothing until they hire another Fairy Mischief."

"Mm-hm." Min-Jun set his beer down. "And when was the last time you dated anyone?"

"Not that long ago..." Taeyang said. "There was that girl from the papercraft store."

"I don't know if it counts as dating if you only saw her once." Min-Jun picked up the television remote and loaded up Netflix.

"We had two dates," Taeyang protested. "And she wanted to introduce me to her friends, it was getting serious."

"And you ended it. Why was that again?"

"We didn't have any chemistry," Taeyang said. "I mean, she was pretty and funny, but I sort of forgot about her once I wasn't looking her in the face."

"Poor forgettable girl. And here you are thinking about the Fairy boy even though he's out of your line of sight…"

"It's not the same thing," Taeyang said. "I work with him."

It's definitely not the same thing. I have a lot of chemistry with Lincoln but it's only in character. Aside from lunch yesterday and training we've barely said three sentences to each other. I can't date someone because I like how he is when I'm pretending to be an evil Lord of Order.

"Okay, I'm just putting it out there," Min-Jun said. "I mean, you sound confused as to why you invited this guy into your spare room, and that's one possible answer."

Taeyang drained his beer. "What are the other possible answers?"

Min-Jun didn't look at Taeyang, he just kept scrolling available shows on Netflix. "Let's see, you had a sudden good samaritan impulse because you're secretly a sweetheart."

"No, not that." Taeyang laughed and helped himself to another beer from the stash under the table.

"Or you're letting the villain thing get to you and you want him close so you can crush his dreams and control him."

"Min!" Tossed a cushion at Min-Jun. "Don't be weird."

Close… well, having him close is rather appealing… but not to crush or control him. It feels like he has no one looking out for him, and I'd like to offer him some support, if I can.

"Oh, or maybe you want some help paying your rent. That's a totally valid reason you might have asked him to stay."

"Huh, yes, let's go with that one," Taeyang nodded. *I hadn't thought about it, but that would certainly be helpful.*

Min-Jun hugged the cushion to him and grinned. "But the very fact that you're looking for an excuse to justify your behavior is very telling to me. What are you not admitting to yourself?"

"I think I should go," Taeyang said, downing the second beer. As he stood up there was a knock on the door.

"My pizza! Finally!" Min-Jun dashed past him to take the pizza and tip the delivery girl. He turned to Taeyang who hadn't moved from beside the couch. "There's enough to share, if you want to stay? I was just gonna watch some episodes of that new fantasy K-drama."

"Sure, why not?" Taeyang sat back down and put all thoughts of Lincoln out of his head. He could clear out the spare room in the morning.

"WHAT IF THIS IS A LARGE AND TERRIBLE MISTAKE?" LINK FRETTED, handing Grayson a box to slide into the back seat of Cillian's extra wide vintage Bel Air. "Like, not just large but gigantic, titanic, bigger than the castle in the middle of the park."

"It's just for a few weeks, right?" Grayson said. Being utterly reasonable and putting Link's back up a little more.

Apparently I just want to worry about this.

"Yeah, it's just for a few weeks, I could have moved in with my folks for that time," Link said.

"And suffered the stupidly long commute and whined at me the entire time," Cillian said. He nudged Link aside and handed Grayson another box. Grayson slid it in on top of the other.

Link chewed his nails, a tic he had for the most part eradicated, unless he was on the brink of doing something even he knew was stupid or under far too much stress. "I don't know. I could manage."

"Link." Grayson turned and smiled his warm, friendly, all-American good guy smile at Link. It shouldn't be as effective as it was. But it made Link feel safe somehow. "It's going to be just fine. Take a deep breath in, and then let it out, with me." He demonstrated a long slow breath and Link did his best to match it.

"Right, okay," Link said.

"Try it again? See, breathing deeply doesn't suck."

"How did you even get that pun in there?" Cillian shook his head and Link's deep breath was disrupted by a surprise laugh.

"Trying not to be a blowhard."

Cillian purposefully ignored the grinning Grayson and patted Link's shoulder. "Just think, you and Taeyang can use some of your downtime to practise and then you can outshine all the other villain and hero pairings."

Link perked up, well aware that of all the things to make him feel better this one was stupidly petty and pathetic, but hey. Whatever worked, right?

"Fairy Gentle will be left in the dust," he said, his voice rather more malevolent than he'd meant it to be.

"That's the spirit. Fairy competition sounds fairy hard." Link groaned at that one. "And Rosa plays Gentle right? She's probably got a very competitive nature."

Cillian shook his head. "What part of stop the puns didn't you understand?"

Grayson shrugged, dusted his hands off and looked back up at the building. "Was there much more still to come?"

"Just my last couple of bags from the bedroom," Link said. "I'll go get them now and follow you guys in my car."

"All right, see you there."

The actual process of moving in wasn't too bad. With Cillian and Grayson helping, and then Taeyang and his friend Min-Jun pitching in, they soon had all of Link's things in his room. Then Cillian and Grayson were hugging Link goodbye, and Link was left with a room full of boxes and out in the main apartment, Taeyang.

He chewed his lip and tried to think of how to make it less awkward. There was nothing. He just had to face the awkwardness head on. He looked around the room, picked up his mirror from where it was propped against the wall and looked at himself. He looked tired, and like he'd spent the day lugging boxes around. At least the late afternoon sunlight was sort of flattering. He set the mirror back down and went out into the living area, where Taeyang was sitting in front of the TV. There was a news show on the screen, but Taeyang turned around as soon as he heard Link.

"Hey, how's it going? Do you want any help unpacking or anything?"

Link swallowed. *Part of me desperately wants to say yes, and have Taeyang take control of the whole unpacking process and tell me what to do and where things should go.*

But that would be weird and kind of wrong, wouldn't it?

Link was a grown up, he had to unpack his own things, and sort out his own room.

"Uh, thanks, but no I think I've got it. Listen, I was just thinking since it's just for a few weeks I'll probably just leave most of my boxes anyway, and I'll stay out of your way, stick to my room, I mean, uh, your spare room. I don't want to be like, in your space more than I have to be."

Taeyang's expression was hard to read but it seemed to be disappointed, or possibly, sad?

Had he wanted to help unpack?

"There's really no need to do that, I don't mind you being out here. In fact I was kind of thinking we could share meals if you were up for that."

"Oh, uh, yeah that sounds great," Link lied. He swallowed and forced a smile. "Thanks, I don't think I'm exactly up for cooking tonight though."

"Yeah I expected I'd do dinner tonight, or we could just order something in?"

"Let's order in," Link said.

He's being so sweet and so kind. So why does my chest feel tight and my throat have a lump in it? What kind of loser cries because someone's being nice to them?

Just act happy, Link. It's all you can do right now.

Link checked his watch. "I guess it's still a little early for dinner, huh? So, I'm gonna make a start on my unpacking. You let me know when you're getting hungry."

He retreated back into the spare room and pulled the door shut, but not all the way. Closing it all the way felt impolite, after Taeyang had been so nice before. And he'd said to let him know, so leaving the door open made the most sense.

Why am I overthinking this so much? Just relax, Link. Relax and focus on your task.

He made the bed up first. That way even if he got nothing else done he'd have somewhere to sleep. Then he opened the duffel bag with his essentials: toothbrush, toothpaste, pajamas, and his secret shame, the Spring the Rabbit plushie that he kept by the bed and sometimes slept hugging.

He stuffed Spring under the pillow, pretty sure he'd need her tonight. Then it was unpacking his clothes into the one, too small chest of drawers. He decided to sort as he went with clothes. He wasn't going to need absolutely everything in the next couple of weeks, so some things came out and went into drawers and some went back into a box to be resealed.

The work was dull, but diverting enough that when Taeyang came to the door, knocking on it lightly, Link had largely relaxed.

"I'm starting to get hungry, shall we order something in now? It'll be a half hour or so before it actually gets here after all."

"Sure, sounds great," Link hauled himself up from where he'd been sitting cross legged on the floor.

"What are you in the mood for?" Taeyang asked, backing into the living room as Link came out.

"I really don't mind," Link said. "What's your favourite local? We can have that."

"Hmm," Taeyang tapped his chin. He looked like he was acting out thinking hard, and it was kind of adorable but also sort of weird. Maybe he was feeling as awkward about this whole set up as Link was? "There's a really good Indian nearby, I could order us a couple of curries and parathas."

"That sounds great," Link nodded. "Oh, do they do that delicious fried onion thing, uh, what's it called. Bhaji? I'd like that too, if they have it."

"I'm sure they do." Taeyang brought up a delivery app on his phone and soon the order was made, bhaji and all.

They both sat on the couch and looked at the TV. "You want to watch anything in particular?" Taeyang asked. "I was just mainlining a Korean drama, but you just moved, you can choose something brainless if you like."

"I uh, well, I've never seen a Korean drama," Link said, genuinely interested. "I'm down for that."

Taeyang gave him a half smile and picked up the remote. "Well, uh, let me choose a good one and we can start from the first episode."

He flicked through a selection of options and settled on one. He set the first episode going and Link sat back. He found the subtitles a little hard to keep up with just at first but soon he was in the rhythm of it and genuinely enjoying the show.

There was a knock at the door and Taeyang jumped up. "That'll be dinner."

"Do you want me to pause this?" Link asked, surprised that the food had turned up so quickly. Or possibly he'd just got wrapped up in the show.

"No, I've seen it before, keep playing."

Link did as he said, and Taeyang brought the containers of food to the coffee table with bowls and forks and they helped themselves.

The curry was delicious, the couch was comfy and the TV show had sucked Link right in. He had soon forgotten how awkward and upset he'd been earlier.

Taeyang took an episode to notice that Lincoln had fallen asleep on the couch. He said something, a joke about one of the characters, and Lincoln didn't respond. Taeyang looked over and he was slumped against one of the cushions, his face soft and utterly free of tension. He looked almost angelic like that, his soft blond hair curling sweetly against the fabric of the cushion. Taeyang had the urge to snap a photo of him to refer back to. Or just to have. He was so pretty.

But what's the best way to wake him up?

If it had been Min-Jun he'd have just shaken his shoulder, or kicked him in the knee. But Lincoln wasn't Min-Jun, and he didn't want to freak him out with something too close in or intimate.

He cleared his throat and then cleared it again, louder. There was no response.

Sighing, Taeyang picked up the remote and switched the TV off, then cleared his throat again.

"Lincoln?" he asked softly. There was no response, he tried raising his voice a little. "Lincoln? Uh. Hey, Link!"

Lincoln startled awake. "Huh? What?" One of his hands flailed, knocking a cushion off the couch. "I fell asleep?"

"You did, yes," Taeyang said, smiling despite himself. Lincoln could be so adorably clueless. "Maybe you ought to go to bed?"

"Right." Lincoln got unsteadily to his feet and pushed a hand through his hair, then yawned so largely it seemed to startle him again. When he was done his eyes widened. "Hey, you called me Link!"

"Well, you weren't responding to your full name," Taeyang looked away. Using Lincoln's nickname felt a little too intimate but he wasn't sure why exactly. Perhaps because Lincoln always used Taeyang's full name.

"It's okay, you can use it, most everyone else does," Lincoln said.

"Well, all right, but if I'm doing that you should also call me Tae," Taeyang said. "That's my nickname."

"Right, thanks." He paused and then said quite deliberately "Tae. Please let me know how much dinner was and I'll pay you back."

"Sure," Taeyang said. "I'll make a running total or something, don't worry about that now. Just go get some rest."

Lincoln looked around, as if he'd lost something or there was something else to say, but then he dropped his hands to his sides and nodded.

"Thanks, Taeyang. I will. I guess, see you in the morning?"

"Yeah, sleep well."

He shuffled off into the spare room, into *his* room and Taeyang tidied up the remains of the dinner, putting the leftovers into the fridge and stashing the paperbag it'd come in into the recycling. He wasn't feeling particularly tired himself, but he knew Lincoln hadn't been sleeping well, so he turned the lights off in the kitchen and lounge and retreated to his room. If Lincoln could at least get a good night's sleep tonight, maybe things would be okay between them.

It'd certainly been very pleasant sitting together and watching TV. More nights like that and they'd soon be friends, Taeyang hoped.

The next day, Lincoln didn't emerge from his room until mid-morning. Taeyang didn't know what to do with himself. He didn't want to make too much noise, because he knew Link needed the rest, but it felt weird to go out and do errands as well. Something in him wanted to be around when Link did actually get up so that he could show him the bread and the toaster and make sure he ate breakfast. Lincoln had brought precious little in the way of food and drink with him the day before. A couple of half eaten boxes of pop tarts and some coffee and that was it.

So Taeyang spent some time on the elliptical machine, which he'd moved into the living area. He spent an hour there, went for a shower and there was still no movement. So Taeyang sat at his small kitchen table and read a book.

Link's door, Taeyang was definitely thinking of it as Link's room, not his spare room already, opened at eleven thirty and a dozy looking Link emerged.

"Good morning!" Taeyang smiled and waved, and then felt like it was overkill so dropped his hand back down.

Link blinked at him and nodded. "Sup."

He went into the bathroom for a while and when he emerged he looked a bit more awake. He sat down at the table opposite Taeyang. "Hey. Guess I really needed that sleep, huh?"

"Guess you did. Are you hungry? What do you usually eat for breakfast? There's bread for toast and there's granola and stuff as well."

Link swallowed and smiled. "Thanks, I'll go shopping later and get some food and stuff. I don't want to just be eating all your supplies or whatever."

He got up and made himself some toast.

SUNDAY WAS A LITTLE TENSE. TAEYANG, *NO CALL HIM TAE*, LINK reminded himself. Tae was being ultra-considerate. Encouraging Link to eat the food he already had, tiptoeing around his own place. It made Link antsy, increasing the feeling that he was intruding.

Link prolonged his trip out to the grocery store just so he could give Tae his own space. Loaded up on breakfast bars, milk and cereal and instant ramen so he could eat quickly and then be out of the way. It was late afternoon when he let himself back in, wincing at how shiny and unused his key looked. Was it possible Taeyang had it cut, or issued just for Link?

Taeyang was on the couch, a notebook on his lap and was writing furiously in it. He snapped it shut when Link came in, which made him instantly suspicious as to what he was writing.

"What's that? Your diary?" Link asked, half laughing.

"Well, sort of, yes," Taeyang said. Link was surprised enough to not have a response right away. Taeyang kept talking. "I started it when I got the job at Fairyland. I thought it'd be useful to keep notes of what worked and what didn't, also to remember things I think of that might be helpful."

"Oh." Link went to the pantry, where Taeyang had cleared a space for him. He pulled out the milk and shoved the bag with all the rest of its contents into the space. He put the milk in the fridge. "Sounds very sensible."

"Why is it that when you say the word 'sensible' it sounds like an insult?" Taeyang said. His voice was closer. Link shut the fridge door to see Tae at the entrance to the kitchen. He grinned, it felt like they were being Order and Mischief, and he knew exactly how to do that.

"Sensible means boring shoes, going to bed early, not indulging in sweets or alcohol and exercising every day."

"Exercising every day and not overindulging is healthy, you know," Tae said.

"Yes, but it's also boring." Link grinned, feeling like he'd won a point. "And boring is bad. Fun is fun."

"All right, but not everything that's boring is bad," Tae said.

"Beg to differ, Tae," Link said. It could have been his imagination but Tae smiled a little wider when he used his nickname. Link filed that away for later, and also the way he felt when he saw Tae's wider smile. That could all be unpacked later. "So, you keep a diary about your job, what do you say about me in it?"

Taeyang's smile turned sly and his eyes narrowed a little. Link guessed that meant he was going to make a joke. "Oh, I write all about how hopelessly infuriating you are, obviously."

Link chuckled. "Obviously. And I'm sure there's lots in there about how handsome and alluring I am, as well."

Taeyang flushed the tiniest bit and he laughed, shaking his head. "Well, I don't need to describe that since I have so many photos of you stuck in there."

Link laughed outright. "Good, that's a relief."

This is good, this is fun. I can cope with this, Link thought. *Maybe the next few weeks won't be too bad.*

A knot in his stomach loosened. Taeyang went to the fridge. "There's probably enough leftovers from last night for both of us for dinner," he said. "I absolutely over ordered last night. You want some?"

"Uh, yeah, that sounds great. I was just gonna make some, uh, ramen, but that sounds a lot better." Link felt unbalanced again and his stomach tightened. *Why did Taeyang have this effect on him?*

"Great, I'll heat it all up," Taeyang said.

"Cool, uh, shall I like, set the table or something?" Link suggested. He didn't want to be a burden and just have Taeyang wait on him. That was the opposite of being chill and relaxing and joking around.

"Sure, go ahead," Taeyang said. "There's some beers in the fridge if you want you could get a couple of those out too."

Link did his best, lining up cutlery and beers on opposite sides of the table, and then fidgeted around with it until Tae brought two plates, loaded with leftovers and set them on the table.

"So uh, I don't mind if you want to do shared dinners," Tae said, picking up his fork. Link bit his lip and loaded up his own fork.

"I'm not much of a cook, I don't know that I can pull my weight if we do something like that." He swallowed and frowned. "I kinda just live off pizza and takeout."

"Well, I kind of like cooking," Taeyang said. "I can do the majority of it and you could pitch in with some money or ingredients?"

Link felt his chest tighten and then release, more complicated feelings washing over him.

He's offering to look after me. Even more than he already has. Oh, wait, does this mean I'm obviously incapable of looking after myself and he just doesn't want me to, I dunno, pass out on the job? Maybe.

"That sounds pretty good," Link said. "But only if it's not a fuss."

"Honestly it's kind of easier to cook for two than it is for one. I often have Min-Jun over because I've cooked too much."

"Okay." Link ate some of the dinner and felt another yawn coming on. He'd slept so well the night before, so deeply and well that it was like his body was hungry for more. Probably he had a sleep deficit to catch up on and his body was impatient to do it. He stifled it in a piece of paratha. But he had other stuff to do before then. "Is there a laundromat in the building?"

Taeyang nodded. "Yeah, in the basement. Coin operated. But it's usually pretty busy on a Sunday night, it might be worth leaving it until tomorrow unless you're really desperate."

"I can probably wait until after work tomorrow," Link said. He didn't hate the idea, it'd mean he got to go to bed sooner. He yawned suddenly, hugely and smothered it with his hand. "Sorry."

"No need to apologize, just get some rest," Taeyang said. "We start show rehearsals tomorrow after all. And it might be quite taxing."

"Ah, I forgot," Link said. Not that he was particularly worried about starting the show, they were usually pretty straight forward lines wise, it'd be the songs and dances taking the most time to learn, but his mind had been so preoccupied with moving he'd straight up forgotten. "How's your dancing?"

"A bit rusty," Tae admitted. "But I used to take jazz and modern dance a few years back."

"You'll be alright, I think," Link said. "You have a dancer's body." He felt his cheeks warm. "Not that I've been like, paying a whole lot of attention to your body or how it looks or anything."

Taeyang smiled. "Thanks, I think. What are the shows like?"

"I've not really been in any before, but the ones I've seen are pretty cute. There's usually kids joining in the songs and dancing in the audience. You can get some really great social media out of it too." He speared a piece of potato and then looked up at Taeyang. "I uh, I don't know if you've looked at your tags or anything? It's still pretty new I guess."

Taeyang frowned and shook his head. "No, I figured I was too new to have much of a following."

"It can get kinda obsessive," Link said. "Me and Cillian, uh, you know, he helped me move yesterday?" Taeyang nodded. "Well, he and I had a bet a while back, that we'd outdo each other on Instagram for this one week. I beat him of course, who gets excited about a pirate?"

Taeyang laughed. "I think quite a lot of people like pirates actually. I mean, especially adults."

Link frowned. "You think?"

"Sure, it's a bit of a fantasy right? Sexy?"

Link got it. People did have fantasies about pirates and princes, princesses too, but not so much about the fairies. He hadn't thought it was something that bothered him, but hearing Taeyang say it he felt crestfallen all of a sudden.

Hurt? Over people in general finding pirates sexy?

Maybe I'm tireder than I thought.

"Yeah, maybe," Link said. He tried to put a positive spin on things. "But my character, yours too, I guess, we're there for the kids. To inspire them, to show them that it's all right to play and have fun. That's kinda more important don't you think?"

Taeyang's eyebrows shot up and he nodded. "Uh, yeah I guess it is. I hadn't quite thought of it in those terms."

Link smiled, knowing it would look a little sad or rueful as he did it. "It's kind of why I've found it more difficult, doing the structured meet and greets. It's not as easy to just go with the flow and play with the kids. I used to play tag all over the forest."

Taeyang took a last bite of dinner. "I'm sorry."

"It's not your fault." Feeling a bit like a jerk and quite dejected by his own words, Link got up and picked up his plate. "Thanks for sorting dinner. What time do we need to leave in the morning?"

"Seven thirty is best to get across town in the morning traffic," Taeyang said. "I can drive if you like, so you can learn the route."

Link knew his offer was sensible but the continual offering to help and take care of things was starting to grate on him and he wasn't entirely sure why. He sucked it up and nodded. "Sure, makes sense."

He stuck his plate and cutlery into the dishwasher.

"Night Taeyang, I'll see you in the morning."

"Yeah, goodnight."

On Monday morning, Taeyang got to see the full glory of Link first thing in the morning.

It turned out that Link was not a morning person. In fact, he was mostly still asleep all through getting up, eating his breakfast granola bar and going down into the car. It wasn't until they were in Taeyang's car and driving that he started to actually seem like Link.

"I love this song," he said, turning the volume on the car stereo up.

Taeyang always plugged his phone in with the aux cord and played whatever his music streaming account suggested for the week.

"Yeah?" he said. He glanced sideways at Link and saw his eyes were actually fully open for the first time that day. He couldn't resist teasing him a little. "Good morning."

"What do you mean, we already said good morning," he said.

"I wasn't sure you'd remember that," Taeyang said. He grinned. "It seemed more like you were sleepwalking than anything else."

"Oh?" Link frowned, looked genuinely confused. "No, I remember."

It was a little awkward after that, and the rest of the drive passed without conversation.

．　．　．

They had been instructed to gather in the rehearsal space, so Taeyang and Link headed through the empty park. The gates would open to the public in another half hour and there was no background music playing. It should have been a bit eerie, by all rights. But instead the atmosphere was one of pleasant anticipation, a present about to be opened.

Link had said a cheery hello to the security staff when they signed in, and he seemed a bit more upbeat all round. Tae decided to reach out to him again.

"I like the feeling before the park opens," Taeyang said. "Like anything could happen."

"Yeah, me too." Link grinned at him and put a little skip in his step.

"Kind of intoxicating getting to see this before anyone else does."

Link gestured with one hand, indicating the cobbles in front of them. "Just think, hundreds, maybe thousands of people will walk down this path today, and over time there's been hundreds of thousands... Millions, billions of people and they were all here to have fun and to believe in magic for just a moment."

Taeyang was genuinely touched by this sentiment. He looked down at the cobblestones and tried to imagine all those feet, old and young and in between. "That's awesome," he said, softly.

"Yeah, always cheers me up." Link stretched his arms up over his head and sighed happily. "That and actually sleeping."

Taeyang watched the arch of his back as he stretched and then looked away. His shirt had ridden up and exposed a little flash of skin, which felt forbidden, or somehow wrong to have seen.

"I'm glad you're sleeping," he said, quickly.

"Me too," Link said. "It's made a world of difference and it's only been two nights."

They went into the rehearsal space to find Lily Ysabel and Julia sitting side by side with large cups of coffee. Lily Ysabel raised a hand in greeting.

"Mondays," Julia said. Link bounced over to them with an infuriatingly cute smile.

"What about Mondays? I feel great!"

Julia groaned and tossed a balled up napkin at his head. "Go be perky elsewhere, I beg you." She turned her gaze to Taeyang. "Please come and collect your fairy, will you?"

Taeyang chuckled, ignored the warm feeling in his belly from Link being described as 'his' and shook his head. "Nope, he's all yours, thanks."

Link pulled a chair up beside Julia's and sat down, tossing the napkin she'd thrown at him between his hand like it was a rubber ball. "What'd you get up to on the weekend, Jules?"

Taeyang realized that this was the Lincoln he'd been expecting right from the start. The worry over his house and living circumstances had really had a huge impact on him. Now he was seeing something closer to what Link was really like. It filled him with happiness in a way that felt a little wrong and almost dangerous.

Because he couldn't get a crush on Lincoln, couldn't fall in love with him. It was just going to mean heartbreak if he did. Lincoln would never be interested in someone like Taeyang. He was too fun, too independent and free spirited. Taeyang would bore him, would have no idea how to keep him interested.

Just have to dismiss all feelings that might be more than friendship. Ignore them. We're going to be in close contact while he's staying with me, so just be careful.

Stefan walked in with Phoenix James and they were all exchanging good mornings when Rosa hurried in.

Arlo opened the back door and came in with a stack of stapled papers, his clipboard and a flustered-looking expression. He looked between all of them and seemed to be counting. "Everyone but Nate?"

"Yeah," Taeyang said. He went closer, holding out a hand to Arlo as he asked "Are those the scripts for the shows? Do you want help passing them out?"

"Yeah, that'd be great actually, thank you. They're named on the front, thanks, Taeyang." He passed over the scripts with the clipboard on top and then took the clipboard back. "If everyone could get their chairs into a circle, we'll do a couple of read throughs this morning, before we get the dancers in and start staging."

Taeyang handed each actor their script as they got the chairs into a rough circle formation.

"Does it matter where we sit?" Lily Ysabel said. "Like, do you want us next to our partners, or?"

Arlo, who had been pulling over a chair for himself, paused for a moment. "Actually, I think it'd be best if you sat across the circle from your partner, that way you can get eye contact if you want it."

"Fine," Julia said. She kicked Lily Ysabel lightly in the shins. "You move."

"Uh, excuse me, but no," Lily Ysabel shook her long curls out over her shoulders. "I'm the villain, you can move."

"Yeah but I've got a raging hangover," Julia said. "Compassionate consideration."

"You kicked me!" Lily Ysabel got up and went across the circle. "I'll do it for you this one time, but know that I'm coming up with some kind of cutting and devastating remark about Constance and getting drunk on a Sunday night."

Julia laughed. "Yeah, yeah. Listen, Lilybel, I'm not Princess Temperance."

"Lilybel?" Link looked up. "Oh my god, that's a super adorable nickname. Can we all use it?"

Just at that moment the door banged open and Nate walked in, both hands full of a big box with a donut shop logo on it. "Sorry! Had to kick the door uh, hands full." Nate grinned at all of them. "I brought donuts!"

"You're my favorite person," Link said. He'd immediately jumped up and was now taking the donut box off Nate.

"Those are for all of us," Nate said. "Not just you."

Link laughed, and it was the free, clear laughter he used in the park when he was playing with a kid as Fairy Mischief. It took

Taeyang a moment to tear his eyes off him, but his attention was pulled by Stefan.

"Hey, uh, Tae, you also have to let go of the script, not just hand it to me and then hold on with a vice-like grip," he said.

Taeyang looked down and realized he'd been frozen in place, holding Stefan's script out and gripping it so tight he couldn't pull it away.

"Right, of course," he let go and looked at the remaining scripts in his hand. Link's, Nate's and his own.

He set Nate's down on the chair across the circle from Stefan's and waited for Link to come back and choose a chair.

Link was busy handing the donuts around, by holding the open box out to each person and saying 'no not that one' if they looked like picking the one he wanted.

Nate took his seat. "Sorry for holding everyone up, I got to drive in today and I couldn't resist the donut shop drive thru."

"It's fine," Arlo said. He helped himself to a plain glazed donut and Link brought the box to Taeyang.

"Donut?"

"Which is the one you want?" Taeyang said, eying the remaining choices.

Link narrowed his eyes and screwed his mouth to one side. "Why do you want to know that?"

"Either so I can avoid it or so I can take it from you," Taeyang said, letting a little Lord Order voice slip in. "But you won't know until you answer me."

Shouldn't be doing this, Taeyang told himself. *This feels too close to flirting instead of just joking around. Got to ignore anything more than friendship feelings.*

Link took a moment to eye him suspiciously before reaching into the box and snatching up the donut with pink icing and chocolate hail on it. "Hah, now it's mine."

Taeyang shrugged and took a chocolate glazed. "This is the one I wanted anyway. Now sit down so we can start."

"You're not the boss of me," Link said. His voice slightly muffled from speaking through donut.

"No, I'm the villain of you. Sit." Taeyang said, taking a seat and setting his script on his lap. Link slunk to the seat opposite and did the same.

"If everyone's ready, let's get started then," Arlo said. "Julia, Princess Constance opens the show, so you're up first."

Julia sighed, set her coffee cup down and flipped open the script, sitting up straight and putting on a gentle soft smile before speaking.

"My, what a simply perfect day here in the Enchanted Forest..."

THEIR FIRST DAY OF LIVING *AND* WORKING TOGETHER HAD GONE well. The drive home from Fairyland had been animated, Link feeling energized by the script and from the bubbling energy there had been in between him and Taeyang as they read their lines. Later in the day, when they'd added movement and stage blocking to the script it'd been even better.

Once they got home though, the energy had changed a little. It was hard to say exactly what had triggered it. Taeyang didn't seem inclined to talk all of a sudden, so Link asked where the nearest gym was and headed out to burn off some energy.

The gym was a block away, and Link paid for a day access pass.

Even though I'm still supposed to be saving money...

He went into the weights room and grinned, seeing a familiar couple of faces at the bench press. Dash was on his back and Nate was spotting for him.

"My two favorite princes," Link exclaimed, walking over to them.

Nate looked over briefly and then went back to keeping a careful eye on Dash as he lowered the weight bar slowly down and then up again. "Hey Link! I didn't know you came to this gym."

"Oh, I don't really," Link said. "Just kinda in the area for a couple of weeks."

"Hi, Lincoln," Dash said. He grunted and replaced the bar on the holder. "Did you want to use this?"

He looked at the number of weights on the bar and shook his head. "Nah, you keep it up, I might just do a couple reps with a kettlebell and then get on the treadmill."

"That sounds good to me," Nate said. Dash sat up and Nate leaned over to ruffle his hair. "You done here, babe?"

"Yeah," Dash said. "I might jump straight on the treadmill. See you over there?"

"Perfect," Nate grinned. "See you in a bit."

Nate and Link made their way towards the racks of smaller weights and the kettlebells. Link selected a smaller sized one and picked it up, rolled his neck and then started to do some lunges. Nate watched him for a moment then started to do the same.

Link was surprised to find he didn't exactly know what to say. He was happy to be spending non-Fairyland time with Nate but he felt at a loss for what to talk about with him. Thankfully, Nate had no such problems.

"How are you finding all this special training?" Nate asked. His eyebrows went up but he had a soft smile on his face, inviting Link to be honest with him.

"It's all right," Link said. "I've kinda been dealing with some life stuff the past couple of weeks so I guess I haven't been concentrating as well as I should have been on it all, but yeah, it's an interesting change of pace." As he said it, he thought longingly of how things used to be. He cleared his throat. "I do still miss just being able to go out and do my own thing though."

"Yeah," Nate said, sympathetically. "I can't imagine. I mean, I never had the freedom that you did. Seemed like you had a ton of fun with it."

"I did." Link sighed.

"But you and Taeyang seem to be getting on really well," Nate said. This time when Link looked over at him he saw a knowing sparkle in Nate's eye.

What does that mean? What's he getting at? Does he know that I've moved in with Taeyang? Even if our relationship isn't like that it must look weird.

"Huh." It wasn't Link's best or most witty response ever, but it seemed to be all he could manage. He set the kettlebell back down and windmilled his arms so stretch his shoulders before picking it back up again.

"Well, it looks that way," Nate said. He set his kettlebell down and ran a hand through his hair. "I mean, you're great in character, obviously, like right from that first improv when the two of you were just zinging off each other. But this morning you were joking around…" His mouth twisted into a small smile. "Flirting, one could even say."

"We weren't flirting," Link said quickly. Definitively. "There's no way."

"Is there no way?" Nate asked. "Okay, I must've read it wrong then."

"Yeah." Link frowned at the floor and switched to squats with his legs spread, the weight held between them. "How are you doing with your partner, er, Stefan?"

"Oh, Stefan's so much fun," Nate said. "He does this bit as Haste, where he turns really suddenly and the robe swirls all around him. And honestly, it's fun playing against someone who doesn't have to be nice all the time, you know? I mean, I love working with Ari, Dash and Greer, but sometimes it all gets a bit same-same. Everyone being so nice and polite and sweet… Stefan can like, tell me I'm reckless and useless and then I can act all incensed and, I dunno man, it's just a great change for me."

Watching Nate talk about it like that was inspiring. His passion for the role, and for the fun of what they were doing, sparked something in Link as well.

"You're right, it is a nice change," Link said. He didn't add *it's kinda sexy too* because well, they were in a gym for crying out loud, but also because then he'd be admitting that Taeyang was sexy and he'd just denied flirting with him.

"The show's gonna be fun too, don't you think?" Nate said. He set the kettlebell down and wiped his forehead.

"Yeah, I think so," Link said. He breathed out and set his kettlebell down as well. "Treadmill?"

"Yeah."

Link went out, which was good.

It gave Taeyang a moment to gather his thoughts, let go of the weird attraction to Link stuff and just focus on what he wanted to be doing. Namely: taking some photos of the latest books he'd read so he could make some social media posts. His accounts had been suffering from lack of attention, since Fairyland had been taking up a lot of his headspace and concentration.

He set up the first book, a romantic comedy about a gay witch librarian in New Zealand, next to the yellow and orange section of his bookcase. He set his phone on a tripod, switched on the fairy lights on the bookcase, and then a light and diffuser to ensure the picture was as perfectly lit as it could be.

He took a few photos, adjusted the position of the book and then took some more.

Then it was time for the next book. Its cover was a Korean literary novel, pale pink with a close up of half a woman's face on it, and he was trying to decide between putting it by the pinks and reds or the blues for contrast when the door opened and Link came in. Taeyang turned to face him, half wishing he could hide all his set up and excuse it away. He started to say something, but the words died in his mouth.

Link's hair was damp, a darker blond than normal, and tousled so it fell on his forehead in a pleasing way. He wore a tank top and soft black workout pants with a white stripe down the side and he looked… Taeyang breathed out. He looked like he'd be very satisfying to hug and snuggle up to right then.

"Hey," Link said. His eyes were on the bookshelf and the lighting. "Oh, you're doing your Instagram stuff? Cool, don't let me interrupt." He crossed the room, his gym bag in hand, heading for the door to his room, when he stopped and gave Taeyang a mischievous smile. "Unless you want some help arranging all your forks in a very specific grid pattern?"

Taeyang's embarrassment was swallowed by irritation and he raised his eyebrows and shook his head. "No, thank you. I can't imagine you'd get it right, anyway."

Link laughed, free and easy, the laugh which had developed the curious ability to snag Taeyang's heart. "Fair enough, I don't think I'd be able to resist setting one on the wrong angle."

Taeyang switched off the lights. "You hungry? I was going to make something for dinner after this, may as well do it now."

"Yeah, starved, to be honest." Link tossed his gym bag into his room and ran both hands through his damp hair. "Can I help?"

"Uh, I guess?" Taeyang went into the kitchen and pulled out the ingredients for fried chicken and a green salad with arugula and pear slices, Link was close behind him. "I'm pretty used to cooking on my own, but… here, you can wash and cut up the pears for the salad."

"Pears in a salad?" Link chuckled. "So fancy."

"It works well with the spiciness of the arugula," Taeyang said. He handed Link a cutting board and the medium sized knife he usually used for cutting fruit and got out some bowls for himself. One for flour, one for panko and one for beaten egg. He took the chicken pieces out of the packaging and started to coat them, flour then egg then panko crumbs, and set each coated one on a clean plate.

Link was suddenly watching over his shoulder. "Is *that* how you get the crispy skin?"

"Yes," Taeyang said. "You can do an extra layer of egg and panko to get it really crunchy."

"Can I have a go?" Link asked. Taeyang hesitated for a moment, and then nodded. "Yes, if you like." He moved aside and washed his hands, leaning a hip against the counter to watch as Link picked up a drumstick and rolled it in the flour, then the egg and then the panko. His face was serious in concentration, a little wrinkle showing on his brow as he carefully laid the chicken down on the plate next to Taeyang's.

Why did I hesitate before saying he could try it? Taeyang folded his arms and breathed out slowly. *Did I think he'd do a bad job? It's not like it matters if the chicken is perfectly coated or not, it just has to be mostly coated.*

No, it was about him. How he looks fresh from the shower, all soft and beautiful.

It was about his proximity to me. He was right there with his breath on my shoulder and I didn't want him to move. I wanted to lean back and feel his chest on my shoulder, his arms going around me.

I like the way his shampoo smells. I caught a whiff of it and I wanted more.

As Taeyang watched Link coat another chicken piece with flour he realized the truth of it all, and it was as sure a realization as he'd ever had. He had to swallow down an exclamation of 'oh of course'. Because he had a crush on Lincoln. That's why he'd invited him to come and stay in his house, and that's why he suddenly got tongue tied or forgot what he was thinking.

I hated the thought that he couldn't sleep, I wanted to help, but it wasn't because of some good, kind altruistic reason. I just wanted him to be safe and happy and… a little bit mine.

He swallowed again and turned away from watching Link's hands, his long, sure fingers turning the chicken so it was totally coated before setting it in the next bowl.

Taeyang pulled a large saucepan out and filled it with an inch of cooking oil and set the element on hot. Then he went to the fridge and opened it.

A beer, I need a beer.

No, wait, that will loosen up our inhibitions. That's not what I need at all.

He pulled out the jug of filtered water he kept in the fridge door and poured himself a large tumbler of it. He took a deep drink.

"Are we doing all the pieces?" Link asked. Taeyang looked back and nodded.

"Yeah, we'll fry it all tonight and then we can have leftovers for lunch tomorrow."

Listen to you, saying 'we' like you're an old married couple. Oh god, I've got it worse than I thought.

"Okay," Link said cheerfully. "Uh, I wasn't sure what to do next with the salad."

Taeyang looked past Link and saw the salad cut into mismatched slices and chunks on the cutting board and sighed dramatically. "Have you not heard of cutting things evenly, Link?"

Link laughed. "No, I haven't. I live to make your life difficult."

"I believe that," Taeyang said. He took out a salad bowl, tossed Link's pear bits in and then tore up some arugula and dumped it on top and seasoned it. He remembered he was cooking for two and added some more arugula. He didn't even know if Link would eat a salad, but you had to have something to balance out the fried chicken.

He grated some parmesan cheese into the bowl, then some roast cashews he had half a packet of from another recipe. Finally he added his favourite store bought raspberry balsamic dressing and tossed it all together with salad servers.

"The oil is spitting at me," Link said. Taeyang looked up. He'd lost himself briefly in the making of the salad and Link's voice startled him, which was very silly since he'd just had a revelation about the man.

Maybe it's my brain trying to preserve me. It should, I can't just fall in love with someone because he needed help. What's that called? Sir Galahad syndrome? He needs rescuing so I'll do it? I'll rescue him and fall in love because of how much he needs me? Problematic.

"Good, spitting is what we want."

"Oh, is it now?" Link drawled. "And here I was thinking guys usually liked me to swallow."

With supreme effort, Taeyang ignored Link's comment and the warmth it brought to his cheeks.

They couldn't fit all the chicken nibbles in at the same time, so Taeyang did them in lots of three, turning them and letting them cook through. Link was fascinated by the process, leaning over to watch and asking questions.

"Have you seriously never fried chicken before?" Taeyang asked.

"No," Link said. "Mom didn't really let me anywhere near the kitchen, and even then I can't remember her ever frying chicken. If we had fried chicken it was bought from a store."

"Huh."

"Where'd you learn to cook?" Link asked.

Taeyang thought back, considering. "Well, some of it was my mother teaching me back when I was a kid, just like, the basics. Then when I was over here, some of the host moms would show me how to make a thing or two. I guess I'm mostly self-taught after that, I just look up recipes online and find things I'd like to make and try them. But the basics came from my mom and my host parents."

"Cool," Link said. "I guess you met some really lovely people through staying at people's homes?"

"Yeah, some," Taeyang said. He felt a twinge of guilt when he realized he hadn't called Tracey for a while. She was practically his second mother, having had him for three of his teenage years before they'd sold their house and downsized. She didn't even know he'd got the job at Fairyland. "Some of the people just do it to rent out their spare room and they're not particularly warm, but some really make you feel like part of the family."

"That's nice." There was a moment's silence before Link spoke again, thoughtful. "Have you ever considered taking on exchange students in your place?" Link asked.

It was an innocent question but it sort of startled Taeyang. "No, I guess I always thought of it as something that couples with kids do, or couples whose kids have grown up and left. I don't even know if they'd let me, single guy alone in an apartment and everything."

"I'm sure the programme screens everyone," Link said. "Could be a good use for your spare room once I'm out of your hair."

Those words set off a confusion of emotions in Taeyang's chest. He wanted Link to stay as long as he wanted, of course, but this was never supposed to be a permanent situation. He huffed, set the cooked pieces of chicken on a paper towel to drain and put some more in. And the idea of taking in some young, confused Korean kid and giving them a home? That was something he had maybe considered in terms of much further down the line. A decade or two away, when he was happily settled with a husband, or partner, of his own, maybe. But not something to think about now. Unless it was?

He wanted to turn to Link and ask him flat out to just stop confusing him. But if he did that, he'd have to explain what it was that was confusing about Link's presence, or Link's words, and that would be ridiculous. It was just a foolish crush, and he didn't need to give it any more thought, let alone words.

"Would you mind setting the table?"

TWO DAYS LATER, ON WEDNESDAY, LINK WAS SITTING WATCHING THE rehearsal of the new villains show. They were in the actual performance space, a small theatre used irregularly for shows or for meet and greets when it rained too hard.

The play was up to the scene where the villains were having a meeting, discussing whether or not to team up and try to take down the heroes together.

Link was sitting beside Rosa, who was deep in her phone, paying no attention to the show.

The scene was a funny one, with each of the villains really hamming up their reasons for hating the heroes, and Link was particularly liking the way Taeyang tossed his head with contempt when he said the words 'Fairy Mischief'. It gave Link a tingle all through his chest.

Perhaps it was because he knew Taeyang better now.

He knew that Taeyang was a kind and generous person who would happily give up his spare room to someone in need, someone he barely knew.

He also knew that Taeyang was concerned about what Link was eating, and had offered to share dinners with him, that Link was eating more vegetables and fresh food than he had in a while because of Taeyang's kind offer.

Living with Taeyang had been unexpectedly relaxing. Link

had intended to lurk in his spare room and stay out of the way, but they'd started watching that show together on Netflix, and Link was addicted. Which meant they'd quickly fallen into a routine where they made dinner together and sat on the couch as they ate, watching the drama unfold. Link hadn't even connected his console to the TV to play games, because he was enjoying the show so much.

Then, when ten o'clock rolled around and it was time to turn in, Link slept better and more soundly than he could ever remember sleeping before. He fell asleep as soon as his head hit the pillow, and slept through the night until his alarm went off.

Even before all the drama with the apartment he'd never been able to sleep the whole night through. He'd wake up when one of his roommates used the bathroom, or when the building made a strange noise settling or sometimes just startle awake from a dream.

And maybe it was just he was making up his sleep deficit, that was definitely a possibility, but he'd slept so well since moving into Taeyang's house that he felt like a new person almost. Five years younger and full of energy.

"What are you smiling about?" Rosa asked, her voice sly.

Link glanced at her, surprised that she wasn't still deep in her phone. "The show's funny," he said.

"Is that all?" She leaned on his shoulder and tipped her head closer to his. "Or are you enjoying watching someone in particular? Don't think I haven't noticed the two of you arriving together in the morning and leaving in the evening."

Link flushed, because actually, he'd assumed no one had noticed that. But evidently that was wrong. "Oh uh, no, it's just that I'm staying in Taeyang's spare room for a bit, until Cillian's apartment comes free."

"Mm-hmm." No one could make those two syllables sound as skeptical as Rosa did then. She poked him in the arm. "You know it's okay to date other staff members, right?"

"Yes, I know that. I've seen Nate and Dash, and Max Jones and Charlie as well," Link said. "And Grayson and my best friend

Cillian, and yeah, everyone knows it's okay. But that's not the point because it's not what I'm doing."

"Okay, Linkie, if you say so."

"I do." Link shook his head. "I'm so not his type anyway." He bit his tongue after that second sentence slipped out, he really hadn't meant to say anything more. The sentence had sounded sad, almost longing.

"How sure are you of that?" Rosa asked.

"Very sure," Link said. "The guy has a bookstagram and makes himself dinner most nights. He cooks extra so he has leftovers for lunch the next day. There's no way I could keep up with that level of organization."

"Oh honey, that is one low bar," Rosa whistled softly.

Don't I know it.

"I know, and my life is pretty much a train wreck. My best cooking efforts are cup noodles and toast with scrambled eggs. So. You see how it wouldn't work." Link swallowed. *He deserves someone so much better than me. Someone with his life together and savings, and a five year plan.*

"All right! Good scene!" Arlo called out. "Ready for the next one, we need Link and Rosa up here for the 'Fairies are Interrupted' scene."

Rosa hopped up and waved at Arlo but leaned in to hiss to Link. "I really think you're selling yourself short, Link. You're cute, funny and great at your job. You've got a lot going for you." Then she turned and practically skipped up at the aisle to the stage.

It shouldn't mean so much to Link to hear her say that he was good at his job. He'd spent so long half heartedly resenting her and her popularity. He'd set them up as rivals in his head, but the fact was he respected her. Respected her approach to the role, the way she connected with guests while playing Fairy Gentle and her attitude out of character as well.

With a spring in his step, Link followed her up to the stage, feeling on top of the world. He hurried up the steps.

"So, there'll be a musical interlude here," the stage manager said from the wings, looking out at Arlo. "It's about twenty seconds, we'll use it to get rid of the evil castle set and bring the forest back in. That will give these two lots of time to get into position."

"Great!" Arlo gave a slightly manic thumbs up in response. Link wondered just how much of their job Lennon had off-loaded to him. All of this, for a start...Lennon had been getting more and more responsibilities since Max Jones had started making changes, so it made sense, but he felt for Arlo having to shoulder so much.

Taeyang was still up on stage, as he and Phoenix James were the two who would interrupt Link and Rosa.

"Nice job," Link said, as he reached the stage. Taeyang stepped to one side and gestured for him to take center stage.

"Thanks, Link," Taeyang said. Link felt tingles at the sound of his nickname coming out of Tae's mouth. "Listen, I was thinking we could stop off at the Asian grocery on the way home and get stuff for hotpot, since you said you'd never had it before. I think you'll really like it."

Link beamed. He had said the food they'd eaten on the Korean drama show looked incredible and apparently Taeyang had remembered, and wanted to introduce it to Link. It was such a sweet and kind gesture that Link spoke without thinking.

"I love you," he said. And once it was said, Link bit his lip, but the fact was he had felt a wave of love for Taeyang and on impulse he'd spoken it aloud. Taeyang looked at him incredulously for a moment, then his expression softened. His eyes crinkled and his mouth began to smile, Link was sure he'd seen it, but it was gone in a flash. Taeyang shook his head and laughed with a touch of nervousness, like Link had made a bad joke.

"Ah, don't be silly, Link, you know I'm just helping you out."

Then Taeyang turned and he joined Phoenix James in their position in the wings.

Link's heart thudded once, quite hard, and his stomach

knotted. He breathed out. He hadn't really just said that, had he? And meant it?

Surely it was better if he meant it as a joke, the way Taeyang assumed he had. He cleared his throat and took his mark on the stage, hardly hearing Arlo's directions.

Did I mean it?

Do I love him? He's sweet and kind and funny and he's being so lovely to me… it could be that I love him.

Or am I just so pleased to have a house and someone cooking for me that I fooled myself into thinking it's love?

THEY WERE ON THE NEW PARADE FLOAT, AND THE MUSIC HAD DONE the tonal shift meaning it was time for the villains to be 'winning'. Taeyang, as Lord Order, was about done with Link's smugness and had been getting more and more irritated with him, he was pleased now he got to turn the tables on the Fairy.

"Now I have you, Fairy Mischief! You've meddled with my plans once too often!" Taeyang projected in his best Lord Order voice, and pushed Link back against the flagpole in the center back of the float. It flew the Order symbol in purple and green. Link grabbed his arm with both hands and glared up at him through his floppy blond hair.

"Your plans are pointless, there's no sense in making things ordered when they don't have to be! You're trying to control too much!"

Taeyang had rope in his hand and he grinned, pulling Link's hands behind the pole, where Link obligingly held them still so he could loop the ropes around him. He let his anger and annoyance at Link guide his actions. He didn't know what he wanted, but it wasn't Link running about and messing with his rather well structured way of life.

"It's just for show, remember" Link hissed through his teeth. There was a slight flash of panic in his eyes as Taeyang pulled the rope tight, letting it cut into the skin on Link's arm just a tad. "You don't have to really…"

"I have to make it look convincing," Taeyang snapped under his breath. "For the audience." He spared a glance to the crowd at either side of the road but it was just trees, lots and lots of Enchanted Forest trees. Perhaps they were all alone?

"You don't have to cut off my circulation." Link struggled against the ropes, but it was actually too late, Taeayng had knotted them and he couldn't get free. Something in Link's face relaxed then, knowing he was trapped, and his mouth opened slightly, as if inviting Taeyang to kiss him. His eyes had gone all 'come hither'.

It was incredibly arousing, Taeyang felt warmth pooling at the base of his stomach and he cleared his throat. They were performing after all. Link seemed to remember at the same time and he pushed his chin up in an adorably defiant way.

"You'll never get away with this, Lord Order!"

"I think you'll find I already have," Taeyang said, his voice loud and ringing impressively. Link's mouth opened again and Taeyang felt drawn to lean in and kiss him, kiss him hard so he'd know who was in charge. Tug on the ropes he'd wound around his body and hear him whining and whimpering with need. He moved closer, claimed Link's mouth with his and tasted the delicious sweet flavor of him.

Taeyang woke with a start, more aroused than he'd felt in a very long time, and sweating with need. There was a small mercy that it hadn't been a wet dream, but now he had a situation to deal with.

He glanced at the time on his phone and swallowed. Half an hour before his alarm was due to go off. He switched the alarm off. He could take care of it now, in the bed, or go take a cold shower.

He got to his feet, grabbed his bathrobe and held it in front of him as he made his way to the bathroom. Thankfully Link's door was shut and there was no sound coming from there, although it was a perfectly natural thing to have happen first thing in the morning, Taeyang thought it was best if Link wasn't thinking about him that way.

He locked the bathroom door behind him and stripped off his pajamas, turned on the shower and hopped in before it had properly warmed up. The shock brought a little relief and he sighed, letting the water run over his body as it steadily got hotter.

That dream was... unexpected.

Or was it?

Link had casually said 'I love you' the day before. But that wasn't... Link said he loved things all the time. It didn't mean he actually for real *loved* Taeyang. Not like... not in the way Taeyang was afraid of.

That was why Taeyang had dismissed him, told him he was just responding to Taeyang being friendly. Then he'd bolted so that Link couldn't say he wasn't joking because somehow that would have been even more frightening, if he'd said that.

On the other hand, if he had agreed that he was joking, Taeyang would have felt absolutely awful, disappointed, and he didn't want that either.

No, they were just friends.

Link was being friendly. Right?

Do we need to have a talk about this? Sit down and ask Link 'what did you mean when you said I love you? Because I do have a bit of a crush but I think it's just because you were so sad and pathetic and I wanted to help, and then I did help, and that felt good.

Could I really say that to him?

It has absolutely nothing to do with the dusting of freckles on his cheeks, or how he looks when he comes back from the gym, or how kind and funny he is. How witty he is when we do improv in character, so fast with a quip that I have to really push myself to keep up.

And it has nothing to do with dreaming about what happens if I try to control him in a... in a sexual manner...

"Oh no," Taeyang said to the bathroom tiles.

When he was done in the shower, he pulled his bathrobe on and went out just as Link emerged from his room, still in soft grey shorts that left little to the imagination, and no shirt at all.

"Morning," Link said, although his eyes were barely open.

"Morning," Taeyang said, and walked far too fast back into the safety of his bedroom.

The drive into work was quiet. Quiet enough that Link asked Taeyang twice if he was feeling all right and Taeyang, who's mind was still swirling with 'what if's and trying to interpret his own emotions found it hard to answer. It was giving him a headache, a thumping ache starting just above his right ear and radiating out, making him feel cranky as well as confused.

"Yeah, fine."

"Cool." Link sounded like he didn't believe him.

Taeyang gritted his teeth, which did little except make the pain worse. He kept his eyes on the road and didn't say anything.

"I might get a coffee before we start, you want one?" Link said, once they'd got through security in Fairyland.

"No, I'm just going to head in," Taeyang said and kept walking.

"Okay." Link's voice was smaller, almost sounding hurt as Taeyang kept moving. He felt a pang in his heart but he didn't want to stop and give in. Whatever was happening between them, he needed to sort out how he felt before they talked. And to sort out how he felt, he needed to talk to someone. Someone not immediately involved.

He swiped himself into the theatre and looked around. Phoenix James was there, sitting in the back and flipping through a script with a bored look on their face. *Perfect.* Taeyang went directly to them and sat down.

"Good morning, Phoenix James," Taeyang said. "Have you got a minute?"

"For you honey, I have five," Phoenix James said, and gave Taeyang a smile he couldn't interpret. It was either sincere but sort of grating, or it was false sincerity. But whatever, Phoenix James had agreed to talk so Taeyang went right into it.

"Here's the thing, Link's been staying with me, and -"

"Oh ho!" Phoenix James closed the script and placed their hands on top of it, half turning to give Taeyang their full attention. "I had sensed a certain frisson between the two of you."

"You did?" Taeyang bit his lower lip.

"Oh yeah, honey. The way he looks at you when you're not looking, and don't think I haven't noticed you watching him in exactly the same way."

"Huh. I guess I didn't realize I was *watching* him in a certain way."

"That's a surprise? Oh dear, what did you want advice on?" Phoenix James patted Taeyang's shoulder in a conciliatory way. "Go on."

"Right, so, uh. He's staying with me while he waits for his friend's place to be free, and we've been eating together, cooking together, and he wasn't sleeping before he came to stay with me but now he is and he's looking so much better and happier." Taeyang swallowed. He hated to think of how dark the circles under Link's eyes had gotten and how hungry he'd looked.

"I had noticed an uptick in his demeanor, honestly, it was a relief," Phoenix James said.

Taeyang breathed out slowly. "The thing is, I think I have a little crush on him. But I don't know if I should trust it."

Phoenix James pulled a face. "I mean, the word crush is a red flag, you know. You think that's all it is?"

"How would I know?" Taeyang said, a tinge of desperation in his voice that even he could hear.

"I guess, time is a good one," Phoenix James said. "In my experience crushes burn hot and intense and then burn out. Give it a couple of days, maybe less since you're living together, you can indulge in all the Linkie time you like and then see how you feel."

"Okay, yes, that's, yeah, that makes a lot of sense." Taeyang sat back in the chair and stared towards the stage. Just lean into his feelings and spend as much time with Link as possible? It sounded very appealing.

"You could also compare it to how you've felt with other people," Phoenix James said. "Like, your last partner, whoever they were, what did they make you feel at the start? How did it go? Sometimes history repeats itself no matter how much we think we've learned."

Taeyang looked back at Phoenix James, whose expression had got more serious as they stared at their hands. "I'm sorry," Taeyang said softly. Phoenix James looked up and shook their head.

"It's fine, I've been single for more than a year now and I'm learning all about me." They smiled again and this time it was definitely sincere, if a little sad. Taeyang leaned a little closer to them.

"Thanks, this has been helpful, I didn't mean to make you y'know, think about bad stuff in the past."

"You didn't," Phoenix James said. "Just, look, before you do anything drastic, picture what you want in the future. Like, a year from now - where are you living? Are you still in this job? Have you got a cat? Is there someone there with you? If so, what kind of person are they? Then do it again for five years from now, and ten. Imagine you're the happiest little Tae you could be, and what is it around you that's keeping you happy?"

"Oh, that's... that's quite the thought experiment." Taeyang rubbed a hand over his forehead. "Okay."

"Yeah, it's gonna take you a half hour or so, and I recommend writing it all down, because it's a trip," Phoenix James said. "I've done it a couple of times and it's legit draining. But useful."

Taeyang nodded and squeezed Phoenix James's hand. "Thanks, really. Can I buy you lunch or something to say thanks?"

"Of course you can," Phoenix James said. "But only if you don't want to spend lunch break gazing into the eyes of the dashing Fae Prince of Mischief." Their gaze slid past Taeyang's face to see Link as he walked in, coffee in hand, waving at Arlo and Lily Ysabel up the front of the theatre.

Taeyang's heart did a little flip of excitement, or possibly nervousness. "I'll let you know."

"You do that, Tae-Tae. Can I call you Tae-Tae?"

Taeyang grinned at Phoenix James. "Only if I can call you Fifi."

Phoenix James burst out laughing. "All right, it's a deal, but only you can get away with that!"

Taeyang laughed as well, then squeezed Phoenix James's shoulder. "See you out there. And really, thanks."

It was bad enough that he'd let the three words slip out, that he loved Taeyang, when he wasn't even sure he meant it. But on top of that Taeyang was being really weird.

First, he'd come up to Link on stage and just kind of stared into his eyes for a moment with a serious intensity.

Link wasn't sure what it meant, was he about to kiss him?

Link hoped not, because he wasn't at all sure he wouldn't kiss him back and then it'd be really awkward for everyone in the theater. Mostly because he wasn't sure if he'd be able to stop kissing Tae once he started. Probably he'd want to kiss him and push him against the wall and pull his shirt up and touch his abs, because Link had seen them and wanted to feel them. And possibly lick them, which would be even more awkward.

But then he'd narrowed his eyes and kind of mumbled something about having lunch with Phoenix James.

"Uh, okay?" Link had said. "Have fun I guess?"

It wasn't like they'd been having lunch exclusively with each other. Obviously, they often had leftovers from dinner the night before, but it wasn't like they were at high school and had to sit at the same table or there'd be gossip or something.

Then they'd got into rehearsals and Taeyang felt curiously distant from Link. His lines came out a little stilted perhaps. But that could have just been because of the script, and not because of Link.

Maybe I should apologize for saying I love you?

Link didn't like to do that though. It had been his truth in the moment. But then if it had made Taeyang all awkward and strange he must be thinking about it.

Maybe it would be worth it if he could clear the air between them.

After they finished for the day and were walking through the bustling dinner time crowds of Fairyland on a Thursday night, Link tried to broach the subject.

"Uh, Tae, I'm sorry if I said something to make you uncomfortable," he said.

"You didn't," Taeyang said. Much too fast. Link swallowed and looked at him, walking alongside him.

"It's just the vibe between us has been kind of… weird, and I wanted to check in that you weren't like, angry with me or something." Link bit his lower lip. He'd just hate it if Taeyang was angry at him. He hated people being angry with him, he had no idea how to deal with it except for immediately apologizing and doing whatever he could to make it go away.

"I'm not," Taeyang said. But his voice was clipped, not warm at all. Link frowned.

"It's okay if you are, I mean, I'm all up in your space and then I said, uh, what I said, about… love…" *why was this so hard?* "But like, I didn't mean anything by it. I mean, I like you, and I am super grateful for everything you've been doing but obviously it's too soon to say…" *no, what are you saying? Backtrack.* Link cleared his throat and then coughed twice, feeling a slight tickle in his chest. "You're a great friend." He finished. It didn't feel like enough.

Tae's eyes cut to the side, looking at Link, and then back to looking forwards. "I'm not mad at you, Link. It's fine. I'm just, uh, dealing with some of my own stuff right now."

"Oh." Link swallowed. Why did it sound like 'some of my own stuff' was code for 'dealing with you'? "Okay."

They made it to the car and Link's eye was caught by the sight of a familiar seafoam green Chevrolet Bel Air. Cillian's car. Cillian would be an escape from Tae's weird-ass vibe.

"Hey uh, I might catch up with Cillian, make him give me a ride home. Okay? I'll see you later on."

Taeyang's eyebrows shot up but Link would have sworn on his mother's life that he looked relieved. "Yeah, of course, you have your swipe card, right?"

"Yeah." Link smiled and resisted an utterly irrational desire to kiss Tae's cheek, then turned towards Cillian's ridiculous vintage beast of a car.

He didn't have to wait long before Cillian himself was approaching him, hand in hand with Grayson. Link felt a faint flutter of jealousy that they had things so easy, to be wandering around with each other. They'd found each other and they were in love and now they were dating, and then even had another boyfriend and soon they'd all be moving in together? It wasn't fair at all.

But he was happy for his friend, so he squashed the jealousy down and pasted on a smile.

"Link, hello," Cillian said. "To what do we owe the pleasure? And why in the name of all that is Holy are you sitting on my car?"

"Hey, Link," Grayson said, giving him a little wave.

"Just thought you could use a little me time," Link said. He hopped nimbly down off the car and grinned.

"You know, usually when people say 'me time' they mean time alone, with themselves," Cillian said. He let go of Grayson's hand to hug Link hello.

Link hugged him tight, then clung to him, suddenly afraid he was losing Cillian somehow.

He closed his eyes against sudden tears. He knew he wasn't losing Cillian though, what was it really about?

He might be losing Tae, and he never even had Tae to start with. Taeyang wasn't his.

Cillian seemed to sense his mood, because he squeezed him a

little tighter and patted his back. "Not that I'm not happy to see you, Link."

This is getting weird, stop clinging to him like a four year old who got lost in the park.

With a force of will, Link dropped his arms. He blinked back the tears that were threatening and tried to ignore the look Grayson and Cillian exchanged.

"Everything okay, buddy?" Grayson asked, his voice soft. Link looked at Grayson's concerned expression, blonde hair and blue eyes and his wide shoulders and felt a wave of affection for the man. It was like being taken care of by Captain America.

"Not, well, things are okay. I just might need to move in a bit sooner, after all," Link said. Use your couch, if that offer's still open."

"Yeah, of course," Cillian said. "I can spend some nights with Gray here and give you some space, even." He put his arm around Link's shoulders. "Taeyang giving you trouble?"

Link looked around, suddenly fearful that Taeyang was watching or could hear them or something, but his car was nowhere in sight, long gone, of course. Why would he wait around for Link when Link had said he'd get home another way?

"No, just, giving me confusion," Link said.

"Get in the car, you can tell us about it," Grayson said, opening the passenger side door for him. Link swallowed and hesitated.

"Don't you want to ride shotgun?"

Grayson shook his head. "I feel like your need is greater right now. You take it." He turned and got into the back seat, to cement his offer perhaps.

Link slid in on the passenger side and closed the door behind him as Cillian started the car. "How about we go for a drink and you can let it all out?" Cillian suggested.

"As long as it's not one of those Irish pubs where they all expect me to drink Guinness," Link said.

"No one expects you to drink Guinness," Cillian said.

"No, I know what you mean," Grayson said. "They have all

the Guinness signs up and it's on the coasters and everything. It puts pressure on a person."

Cillian laughed and pulled the car out from the parking lot. "You two are both ridiculous. But fine, there's a nice German beer garden I know of close by, how about that?"

"Fine with me," Grayson said and Link nodded.

It really was close by, they were there in less than ten minutes. Before he knew it, Link was seated with a stein of ale in his hand and Grayson and Cillian both looking at him expectantly.

"This is still a lot of beer," Link said, stalling.

"It's not heavy like Guinness is though," Cillian said. "Now, what's the problem?"

"It's not even really a problem, really," Link said. Their tender, concerned gazes made him feel like he'd made a mountain out of a particularly tiny molehill. "Probably it's just in my head."

"What's in your head?" Cillian prodded, quite literally, nudging Link in the leg with the toe of his shoe.

"This is a safe, non-judgemental space," Grayson said. "Also we know a thing or two about miscommunication, so lay it on us."

Link smiled at Grayson. On another day, he might be a bit resentful that Grayson was there, intruding on his 'best friend' time but now he was glad of it. Grayson was kind and understanding and warm. He put Link at ease.

"So, Taeyang has been really sweet to me, offering me his spare room and everything. We're watching a streaming show together, sharing meals and stuff. But I dunno, he kind of runs hot and cold. Like, sometimes he'll say nice stuff like I'm doing well at work, or he'll look like he's about to say something and then changes his mind. I don't know where I stand with him. And today it's like he's angry at me but I have no idea why or if I even did anything to trigger it."

Link sighed and sipped his ale.

Cillian grinned. "And why does it matter how he acts to you, how d'you feel about him?"

Link felt his cheeks warm and told himself it was just the beer getting to him. "I really like him, a lot. But he'd never... even if I did try something, he'd never go for someone like me. I'm all... I don't have my life together, and he really does. He likes things to be precise and well, beautiful, and most days I don't remember to make my bed."

Grayson chuckled. "Have you said any of that to him, about how you feel? Or are you just assuming that's how he'd react?"

"I've... told him I like him, that I think he's kind, and I'm thankful he's helped me out?" Link said. He bit his lip. It couldn't be that easy could it? Just talking to Taeyang? "And I kinda said I love you, but it just slipped out and he thought it was a joke."

Cillian and Grayson exchanged a look. "Okay, well, talking things through is usually a good way to clear the air," Grayson said.

"Perhaps you should." Cillian's smile was sympathetic. "He's not likely to read your mind, brother."

"Yeah," Link said. "I wish I could read his mind, it'd make all of this easier. That's why I thought using your couch might be a good plan, then I'm out of his space and we get a little distance, I'm sure he's annoyed with me being around all the time when he was used to living alone."

"Has *he* said anything like that?" Grayson said, his eyebrows raised. Link swallowed.

"Well, no, of course he hasn't." Link sighed. "Okay, I'll uh, I'll try and talk to him. But I can use your couch right? I don't really have that much stuff, the boxes pile up pretty neatly..."

"If you need it, it's yours," Cillian said. "Any time, okay?"

Link felt warmth in his gut this time. An uncertain joy and thankfulness that he had a friend who would care about him so much to agree to such a large favor.

"Thanks." Link drained the last of his ale and wiped his mouth with the back of his hand. "Really, thanks both of you."

"If I can give you one more piece of advice," Grayson said, slowly. His voice had gone softer as if Link was a skittish deer who might bolt at any moment.

Link nodded. "Yeah, go for it."

"Think about what *you* want, Link. Like, are you actually into Taeyang, do you want it to be more than friends? If you spend some time really examining yourself, you'll see the answer, and then that can guide your actions."

"You make it sound so simple," Link said, and Cillian laughed.

"It really is that simple, and that hard," Grayson said. "Just, try your best not to assume what he's doing or saying, for a start. Then try and listen to yourself, to your heart. What do you really want?"

Link nodded, feeling close to overwhelmed. His emotions were so close to the surface, so raw from the conversation that he was worried he might burst into tears. And why? Just because Grayson was being so kind and empathetic?

How pathetic am I? I'm practically in love with Grayson now because he's being nice. What do I really want? I want someone to hold me and keep me warm and safe and tell me everything's going to be okay.

Do I want a boyfriend or a parent?

Link shook his head and swallowed down the lump, forcing a smile and letting go of the sudden fear and rawness. "Okay, yeah. I'll try."

Cillian clapped Grayson on the shoulder. "Good work, babe, you got through that whole conversation without punning."

28 / TAEYANG

TAEYANG HAD MADE DINNER, HE'D MADE ENOUGH FOR LINK AND himself out of habit, and then sat by himself eating and feeling out of sorts. Link had been so abrupt at the end of the day, although Taeyang had been so wrapped up in his own thoughts perhaps it was understandable.

He was finishing up his yakisoba when his phone buzzed, Link's name flashed up on the screen.

Hey Tae, just thinking I might use Cillian's couch, move out on the weekend and give you your space back

Taeyang's mouth went dry and he read and re-read the text, trying to make sense of it. He'd give up the comfortable spare room to sleep on a couch? Why?

Have I been that awful to him? I thought I'd done everything right, made him feel welcome... maybe I'm doing too much? Babying him? No, I never got the impression it was a bad thing.

Taeyang sighed and started to compose a message back.

There's no problem with you using my spare room, it's a lot more comfortable

He stared at the words and deleted them out. They were so cold and they didn't address the root of Link's message. There was something happening that Taeyang didn't understand. He tried again.

Are you okay? Please let me know if my behavior is making you uncomfortable in any way.

He looked at what he'd written. It seemed all right, but maybe it was too formal still? Maybe he should just call Link and talk about it. That seemed better. He sent it and then sent another one quickly after.

Do you want to talk? I can call or we can talk when you get home.

Link responded a long minute later.

Yeah, let's talk when I get home.

I'll be there in twenty minutes or so

Taeyang got up and tidied away his dinner dishes, leaving a plate out for Link in case he hadn't eaten.

Talking is good, he thought. *Talking is what I wanted to do, after I'd had some time to think about how I feel and what I want. Have I done that? I've brooded on it all day, but I don't think I've come up with solutions.*

He sighed and stacked his plate in the dishwasher. He knew that the apartment felt very quiet and empty right then, with Link out. He didn't like the quiet. It felt like his footsteps were echoing and reminding him just how alone he was. He thought back to his conversation with Phoenix James.

"Picture what you want in the future," Taeyang said, softly to himself. He went to sit on the couch and give this some proper thought.

Okay, so in one year. Let's start with one year from now, it'll be easiest. I want to be in this apartment, it's very conveniently located and I like being close to Min-Jun. I don't need more space or anything so yes, I'll be living here.

I'm still friends with Min-Jun of course. Maybe I've been to visit my folks in Korea as well.

My love life... well, in an ideal world, I'd like a happy, steady boyfriend who I can rely on. Someone funny and clever and cute. Someone who complements me, doesn't do all the same things but has respect for my hobbies. I couldn't be with anyone who didn't understand what working at Fairyland is like, either.

And for work? I'd still be working at Fairyland. I really like this job.

He realized he had his notebook for Lord Order notes nearby so he picked it up, flipped to the back page and made a quick list.

- FAIRYLAND JOB
- STILL LIVING HERE
- TRAVEL?
- BOYFRIEND

His pen dug into the paper on the d of boyfriend and he thought about the list he'd made. And his earlier thoughts of what he'd want a boyfriend to be like.

Link was clever, witty and funny and he was definitely cute. Even when he didn't have make up on he was golden and sparkly and handsome. He understood about working at Fairyland, better than Taeyang did because of his years of experience.

And more than that, you had a dream about him. You're missing him right now because he's out and you're not. Maybe Phoenix James was right and I ought to just tell him everything, spend a whole lot of time with him and see what happens.

Assuming he's into that idea, of course.

That's what we'll need to talk about.

He looked over his list and then closed the notebook, setting it back on the small table beside the couch and checked the time. It'd been twenty minutes.

He looked at the door in case it was about to open and Link would walk in. It didn't. He didn't.

Taeyang got up and went to the kitchen to boil some water. Maybe the conversation would go better with some tea or coffee. He pulled out two mugs and set them ready, went to the cupboard and pulled out his favorite green tea and lemon blend. He had no idea if Link would be into that, so he got out the coffee as well.

The door opened, startling Taeyang even though he'd been expecting it to open and waiting for Link to come home. He turned, heart in his mouth.

"Hi there," Taeyang said, then winced at how stiff that had sounded.

"Uh, hey," Link said. He smiled but it hadn't reached his eyes. He looked tense. Not as tense as he'd been when he'd been searching for a new apartment but Taeyang recognized the tension in his jaw.

"Would you like tea? Or coffee?" Taeyang said. Link toed his shoes off by the door and walked into the kitchen, his hands buried deep in the pockets of his jeans.

"Uh, yeah tea sounds nice, what kind are you making?" He leaned over the tin Taeyang kept the green tea in and sniffed.

"Green tea with lemon."

"Sounds great."

Taeyang inhaled, getting a whiff of Link when he did, since Link had moved in so closely to him to check it. The scent of him sent all sorts of feelings through Taeyang, but the chief among them was a need to grab him and squeeze him tight. He took a half step back so he didn't do that and instead made them both tea.

"Thanks," Link said. Then he turned on his heel and looked Taeyang in the eye. "Hey, if you need me out of your hair it's okay to say it."

Taeyang shook his head and handed him a mug of tea. "I don't need you to move out. I…" he hesitated, his heart thumping, but hey, if they were going to have this conversation they needed to have it honestly. He had to be open and honest with Link. "I've actually really liked having you here with me. And just now, when you weren't home, the place felt horribly empty and quiet and I missed you." He swallowed and looked into his tea. "Shall we sit down?"

"Yeah, okay," Link said. He led the way to the kitchen table and they sat facing each other. Some of the tension had gone from Link's jaw and instead he was smiling softly. His eyes turned sympathetic. "I guess I just felt a weird vibe from you today, like you didn't want to talk to me, I thought maybe I'd made you angry or something. So, I'm sorry. Whatever I did to piss you off,

I'm sorry. If you could tell me what it was, I won't do it again on purpose."

"I'm not angry at you. I just uh," *how honest is it good to be here? There is definitely such a thing as too honest, right?* "I had a strange night's sleep, a weird dream, and then I…"

He trailed off. Link tilted his head to one side. With his hands wrapped around his cup of tea and his handsome face looking intrigued and confused he'd have made a perfect photo. Perfect for uploading to instagram with a humblebrag tag about how handsome a boyfriend he made.

"I don't think I follow," Link said. "A weird dream? Like a nightmare?"

Taeyang's cheeks burned and he shook his head. "Not a nightmare, a dream about you. It gave me… feelings." *Okay, here we go.* "And I just. I have feelings for you, Link."

"You do?" Link's eyes widened and his shoulders tensed. He coughed once and took a quick breath. "What kind of feelings are we talking about here?"

"Like, good feelings. Maybe, it's maybe I have a bit of a crush on you," Taeyang admitted. He was reminded horribly of Valentine's Day at middle school and offering a boy called Elton his heart. It had been so impossibly awkward. He cleared his throat. "So if that makes you uncomfortable then I guess I understand you'd want to move out."

"I, no. It doesn't make me uncomfortable." Link set his mug down and relaxed into the chair, his body going a little more loose and liquid. He smiled softly and Taeyang's heart dared to hope. "To be honest, I have a bit of a crush on you too, but I was sorta worried it was just because you're like, being so nice and kind and taking care of me. I have some baggage, some stuff from when I was a kid, about being taken care of."

Taeyang's heart thumped. "Oh? Is it a bad thing, being taken care of?"

Link shook his head and his strawberry blond hair fell over his forehead, begging for Taeyang's hand to brush it gently back. "No, it's a really good thing, and that's why I kind of don't trust it, trust my feelings about it, because I love it so much. I dunno, I might fall in love with anyone who took care of me, even if they just meant it as a friend, you know?"

Oh.

"Oh, I see." Taeyang laughed, a sudden sound that he didn't really feel but did to break the tension. "Funny, because I was sort of worried that I was into you because you looked so needy, so in need of care, and I liked being able to give it to you."

Link took a deep breath and bit his lower lip. "Okay, so where does that leave us?"

"I honestly don't know," Taeyang said. He picked up his tea but continued talking instead of drinking. "I mean, if we're both afraid that the feelings are just because… just because I offered you my spare room, then maybe it's better that we don't act on them."

It was hard to say, because it made him feel like he'd lost something precious, but part of him was sure it was the right thing to say. The honorable choice. The correct way to treat someone he cared about.

Link's eyebrows pulled together and his eyes went large and, well, sad, which almost made Taeyang take it all back, but before he could, Link spoke again.

"Yeah, that sounds really sensible." He sounded as disappointed as Taeyang felt. "Maybe once I've moved out we can… see how we feel, though."

"Sensible means boring shoes, going to bed early, not indulging in sweets or alcohol and exercising every day." That's what he'd said. Link hates sensible, but here he is agreeing to it. But I don't know if there's any better way to handle this.

Taeyang nodded. "Listen, there's really no need to go early. Wait until the new place is ready for you and stay until then, okay? I hate the thought of you losing sleep again, especially if it's just because you're sleeping on an uncomfortable couch when you don't have to be."

Link smiled and sipped his tea. "Yeah, okay." His smile turned a bit more mischievous. "You gonna tell me what happened in this dream you had about me?"

Taeyang shook his head, absolutely determined. "Nope."

"Aw, go on."

"Not a chance."

"How hot was it? Was I naked?" Link leaned forward on the table. "Come on, you can tell me, we're friends."

Taeyang got up from the table, avoiding Link's gaze. "Are you hungry? I've saved you some yakisoba."

THE MOOD IN THE APARTMENT WAS PRETTY RELAXED AFTER THE awkwardness of the talk, and Link was grateful for it. The yakisoba was delicious and they watched another episode of what he was quickly thinking of as 'their show', carefully sitting at either end of the couch and not touching.

When they turned in for the night, Link made a lighthearted joke about seeing Taeyang in his dreams and was rewarded with a bit of a blush.

In the morning they drove into Fairyland together. Link had considered offering to drive but his car was such a wreck compared to Taeyang's, it just didn't make sense. He was feeling keyed up as well, antsy and impatient, and he wasn't entirely sure what was causing it.

Maybe it's the idea that Taeyang's having feelings for me? It's kind of, no it's definitely exciting. But nothing's going to happen there, not for a couple of weeks, and even then maybe not. Just because there's a crush doesn't mean it'll last after all.

"Looks kinda like it might rain," Taeyang said, interrupting his train of thought.

Link hadn't noticed, but now, looking up at the sky, he had to agree it had that kind of look to it. It's not like it never rained in California, but it was rare enough to remark upon.

"Huh, hope it's not too heavy. The park gets so humid and gross when it rains," Link said. "And the guests get cranky."

"I can imagine," Taeyang said.

Their schedule for the day was a morning of meet and greets and then show rehearsals all afternoon, so if it was going to rain, Link hoped it was in the afternoon. Getting caught in the rain would be no fun.

They were halfway through their first scheduled meet and greet when the sky darkened. It happened very quickly. Freddie and his daughters had come into the park and Link had been excited to talk to them from the moment he saw them in the queue. Freddie was wearing a plaid flannel over an old rock band T-shirt, and Jemima, Stella and Navi all had jackets over their frilly skirts and dresses. It was cold, Link realized, his shorts weren't doing much to keep his legs warm, although he was sure it had been warm earlier, even ten minutes before.

Stella was hurrying forward to hand something to Taeyang and Navi was skipping towards Link. He was in the act of crouching when he had an urge to cough. He cleared his throat but the feeling wouldn't go away.

Navi was babbling excitedly, telling him about the new coloring book she'd got with Fairyland characters in it and Link felt a tickle in his throat. The cough wouldn't be dismissed so easily.

"'Scuse me," he said, then turned bodily away, raised his arm to his mouth and coughed into his elbow. But it didn't feel like that had removed the problem. He still needed to cough. He coughed again and felt the old, familiar tightening in his chest with a sick dread.

Oh fuck, not now. Asthma again? After all these years? Why right now?

"And the Sparkles the unicorn is in a field with all these flowers, and I'm going to color each of them a different color so they look like wild flowers in a meadow," Navi said.

Link cleared his throat again and swallowed hard, hoping that he could will the asthma attack away. He swallowed again and glanced at Taeyang, who was talking to Stella but glanced over and met his eyes, a clear question in his expression.

Link shook his head slightly, turned away and coughed into his elbow again. This time it wasn't just one cough, if it was a few in succession and Link knew with a horrible certainty that he couldn't will this away.

He needed an inhaler, and warmth. He got to his feet, still coughing and looked pleadingly at Taeyang.

"Hey, buddy, are you all right?" Freddie asked. "Navi, step back a little, I think Fairy Mischief might need a moment."

Link glanced down to see Navi's expression fall from happy excitement into something more like fear. "It's okay," Link tried to say, but he coughed into it instead. He couldn't breathe out properly.

It had started to rain, fat, heavy drops that had people pulling out umbrellas.

Link's mind raced. Rain, sudden drops in temperature, yes, those were triggers. This was really happening.

He cast around for the security staff sent out for them, tried to communicate with his eyes. Then he felt a warm hand on his shoulder.

"Mischief, are you ill?" Taeyang said. He felt another hand on his hip, and then both those hands were propelling him towards Francisco, who was speaking rapidly into his headset. Link managed a nod, closed his eyes and coughed again, this one was so intense it felt it was tearing at his throat.

This is bad, this is really bad.

"Apologies everyone," Taeyang said, in his perfect Lord Order voice. "For the sake of everyone we shall remove Fairy Mischief from the area and take him home, it appears he's allergic to well behaved people."

Freddie pulled his girls against him, creating a clear path. With Francisco on one side and Taeyang urging him steadily forward on the other side, Link made his way towards the nearest staff only path.

I can't get enough air, I can't breathe in, this is bad this is bad this is bad.

Taeyang's heart was pounding and he felt like he could see and hear everything with more clarity than normal. The second Link's step faltered, he wound his arm around his waist and took some of his weight.

"It's all right, I've got you," he murmured. Just at first he'd thought Link had a frog in his throat, but then the coughing got worse very quickly and he remembered one of their earliest conversations. They'd been talking of their childhoods and Link had said *"I was sick quite a bit with asthma"* That's what this was, an asthma attack. He had to do something about it.

"Francisco, it's asthma," Taeyang said. "He'll need an inhaler. Do you have one in your gear, Link?"

Link shook his head, his face had turned red from the coughing but it was clear he wasn't getting enough air into his lungs.

Francisco spoke rapidly into his headset and nodded. "We have them in first aid. We'll get him inside and then someone from the med staff will come with it."

Taeyang looked around, not seeing the staff only path, but following Francisco as quickly as possible. He was striding ahead, assuming they were behind him. Link coughed again, and Tae could feel it shaking his body.

Without thinking, Taeyang scooped Link into his arms. Link,

even though the coughs, looked surprised and his hands plucked at Taeyang's coat. It wasn't exactly the easiest thing Taeyang had done, but Link didn't weigh much and he was confident he could carry him a short distance.

"Don't -" Link's sentence broke into coughs and he shook his head, his eyes closed.

Francisco turned to wait at the entrance to the staff only path, and when Taeyang followed him it was just a quick walk to the back entrance to Wardrobe. Francisco held the door open and Taeyang carried Link inside where it was warm and welcoming.

"We need a chair!" Francisco called into the building and Teddy was there in an instant.

"Here, bring him here, there's a chaise," Teddy led Taeyang a short distance and yanked a blanket off an ancient looking chaise. Taeyang laid Link down on it, where he immediately sat up, bent forward, coughing still.

"Where's that medicine?" He demanded, whipping around to look at Francisco.

"Med's nearly here, they said rubbing his back might help, wide circles." Francisco didn't immediately make a move to do that, seeming to defer to Taeyang. *Just as it should be, I know him best and he's my fairy.*

Taeyang perched on the edge of the seat and placed his palm on Link's back, rubbing circles. "It's going to be all right, someone's nearly here," he said, softly, struggling not to wince with every new cough that wracked Link's body.

A woman in a red shirt with a white cross on it burst in with an inhaler with a long see through plastic chamber attached to it. Taeyang moved back, but kept his hand on Link's shoulder, as she crouched in front of him and brought the hard plastic tube to his mouth.

"Here you go, hon, just take a puff of this, remember how?"

Link opened his mouth and once the chamber was in place she gave him the medicine. Taeyang fancied he could see the cloudy stuff inside, being sucked into Link's mouth. Imagined he could see the way the vapor moved into Link's airways, into his lungs.

He didn't imagine the almost instant relief it gave Link. He sat up a little straighter, his face relaxed a little bit.

"That's it, take a few breaths," the medic said. "Now exhale everything and I'll give you another puff, ready?"

In just a few moments, Link was breathing a lot closer to normally. He still coughed every now and then but it wasn't the frightening type any more. The medic sat back, watching him as he leaned back on the cushions of the chaise and the rise and fall of his chest became regular.

Taeyang realized he was still holding onto Link's shoulder, squeezing it as if he was holding him together. He loosened his grip and was about to take his hand back, but Link's shot up and closed on his wrist.

"Stay," Link croaked.

Taeyang gripped him a little harder again. If Link needed him then he was going to stay right where he was.

The Medic watched Link for a moment. "Do you need more? We can do four doses if needed."

Link shook his head. "M'okay, I think." He tipped his head back like it was too hard to hold up and groaned. "That sucked."

"What do you need?" Taeyang said.

"A drink of water, maybe?" Link said. Francisco nodded at Taeyang and went to the little food and drink station at the back of Wardrobe, returning a moment later with a bottle of water. He handed it to Link, who opened it with a trembling hand and took a swig.

"Have you got an inhaler at home?" the medic asked. Taeyang realized he hadn't even looked at her ID to see her name. It was Judy. Link shook his head.

"No, I mean, if I do it's probably a decade expired." He smiled, tight and mirthlessly. "I haven't needed it."

"You can take this one," Judy said. She pressed the inhaler and the chamber into Link's free hand. "Mr Jones has put a lot of money into the medical department, we have spares. I know he wouldn't want us sending you home with nothing."

Link coughed again but it wasn't what Taeyang thought of as one of the 'dangerous' coughs. "Sending me home?"

"Yeah, I'd like you to get home as soon as possible and rest for the remainder of the day," Judy said. "And bundle up, it's chilly out."

"There's some sweats of mine he can borrow," Teddy offered.

"I'll go get his things from the treehouse," Francisco said. Without waiting for an answer, he jogged off, speaking rapidly into his earpiece about what was happening.

Arlo burst into Wardrobe before Francisco returned. Judy was packing up and moved sideways, to get out of his way. Arlo crouched beside the chaise and touched Link's arm, concern written all over his face. Link gave him a sad smile.

Taeyang stamped down on an irrational desire to tell everyone to back off and give Link some space, which came from a fierce sense of protectiveness threatening to overwhelm him. He felt like a wolf with a wounded mate, but they'd had that talk, about not doing anything until they weren't living together, so he staved off the urge to growl at the others and bit his tongue instead.

"Link, I can't believe this happened, are you okay? We should have called you all back in as soon as it started to rain."

Link shook his head. "It's fine, I've been out in the rain before, a bunch of times. I don't know why today is different."

"Sometimes it's an allergy that can trigger an attack," Judy piped up. "Or if you've been under stress your immune system gets weaker than it was."

"Oh," Link's face fell. "Stress. Right."

"I've recommended he take the rest of the day off sick," Judy said.

"Oh yeah, of course," Arlo said. "And if you need to take Monday as well, it'll be fine. Did you drive in or?"

"I drove him," Taeyang said. "He's staying with me right now, so I can take him."

"Oh, great, thanks Taeyang. Don't worry about coming back in, either, you can both take the afternoon off, paid. It's no problem at all."

Taeyang nodded. "Thanks."

"Okay, if you're feeling alright for now I'll be going," Judy said. "Keep your chest warm, rest up and you should be feeling better in no time."

"Thanks, Judy," Link said. "Really."

Francisco walked in with Link's duffle and handed it to him. Link started to get up, Taeyang was there with a hand on his elbow, assisting him. "Can I use your changing room, Teddy? I'd rather not wear the costume home under my sweats."

"Yeah of course." Teddy said.

"Do you need any help?" Taeyang asked.

Link gave him a look that was partially confusion, partially amusement and a touch of annoyance. "Uh, no, thanks, I got this. I'm actually okay now, just feeling wiped."

Okay, overreacting, he had an attack and he's recovering. He doesn't need to be babied. I need to back off.

"Right." Taeyang felt his cheeks warm and stepped back. "I suppose I'd better get changed as well then. I'll be in the Treehouse…" he was going to ask one of the others to escort Link over when he was ready but that felt like it was going to overreaction territory again so he cleared his throat. "Meet you there?"

"Yeah."

Taeyang had finished dressing and was pacing the Treehouse, trying not to worry that Link had been struck with another attack or something worse when the door opened and Link and Francisco walked in. Link looked somehow smaller than normal in his oversized Fairyland hoodie, and Taeyang's heart warmed to see him again.

"Ready to go?" he asked and Link nodded.

"You really didn't have to walk me over, but thanks."

"Take care, Link," Francisco said. He gave Link a quick one armed hug and was gone.

Link smiled at Taeyang. "Shall we then?"

Taeyang twirled his car keys on his fingers. "Absolutely."

"It looks like it's stopped raining at least," Link said. Taeyang walked behind him as they left the Treehouse and took the staff only path towards the main entrance of the park.

"That's something," Taeyang said. He watched Link's back and the winking Sparkles the Dragon printed on the hoodie. "I'm glad you're alright." His voice came out softer than he'd meant it to, warmer, more... vulnerable.

"Well, with a big bad villain fussing over me there was really no other option, was there?" Out in the park he paused, waiting for Taeyang to catch up so they could walk side by side.

"You scared me," Taeyang said. "And you were having trouble walking."

"And you can bet that as soon as I'm home I'm looking up social media to see all the dashing photos of you carrying me in your arms like I'm your swooning princess."

"Oh, I didn't think of that."

Link chuckled then coughed once into his elbow. Taeyang moved closer in case Link needed him to rub his back again. "It's all right, it just means that Fairyland theme park fans are going to be shipping Fairy Mischief and Lord Order all over the place."

"Oh..." Taeyang found he didn't hate the idea. In fact, he could see the appeal of the villain and the hero hooking up.

Especially after that dream I had... Maybe I should look into the world of Fairyland fanfiction...

Link laughed as he let himself into the car. Taeyang found the sound of Link's laugh sent warmth all through him. It relieved the knot in his stomach, which he hadn't even realized was bothering him, and he breathed out, relaxing into the driver's seat. He glanced over to ensure Link's seatbelt was on before starting the car and driving them home.

Once they were up in the apartment, Taeyang looked at Link and clapped his hands together.

"Right, what do you need? Do you want to lie on the couch

with a blanket, or go to bed? I can make you noodle soup if you like, it'll make you feel better. Or I can just do tea, or, like a hot water with lemon and honey in it? What would you like?"

Link opened his mouth then closed it again. His hands were in the front pocket of the hoodie, and he looked younger, far more defenceless than Taeyang had ever seen him before. It made Taeyang want to bundle him up in a blanket and hide him away from the rest of the world.

"I guess couch and TV is probably what I want," Link said, slowly. "That was a lot of decisions. Um. Are you making soup for yourself as well?"

Taeyang nodded. "Yeah if I make it, I'll do a big pan of it, there'll be enough for both of us and Min-Jun as well." He nudged Link towards the couch, and Link went willingly enough and sat down, pulling his knees up to his chest.

"Noodle soup sounds really nice, thank you."

Taeyang handed him a soft woolen throw blanket and then looked around for the remote.

"It's fine," Link said. "I can find it myself."

"But you don't have to," Taeyang said. "You can just sit back and relax and breathe, in *and* out, and rest."

Link's expression flashed through angry and confused and then his face crumpled and to Taeyang's consternation, tears started to overflow his eyes and streak down his cheeks.

"I'm sorry," Taeyang said, instantly. "Am I being overbearing? I'll back off if you need it."

Link shook his head. "No, I just feel... everyone's making this huge fuss over me and I didn't mean to... I feel bad about it."

"Okay, I know you said you had being taken care of issues, but you definitely don't need to feel bad about getting sick."

Link's face crumpled a little. He stretched his legs out on the couch and opened his arms for a hug. Taeyang didn't hesitate, he leaned in and hugged Link tight.

LINK HELD ONTO TAEYANG AND SOBBED. HE COULDN'T HOLD ANY OF it in. His tears were flowing and all his emotions had come to the surface, leaving him raw and panicky.

His fear over the asthma attack, his attraction to Taeyang, which had only increased since he'd swept in like a hero and scooped Link up and carried him to safety. He'd felt so protected, so secure in his arms.

On top of that, the vague fear that he'd ruined something by showing weakness in front of park guests, that he'd somehow colored or ruined the kids' perception of who Fairy Mischief was. And then there was all the stress over his house, and moving, and should he stay here with Taeyang or not?

It all flowed out of him in sobs that shook his ribs, and made him nervous in case they brought on another attack. Taeyang was half in his lap, obviously trying not to put any weight on Link's torso but holding him securely. Those strong arms made Link feel something he hadn't felt in a long time. Like he was home.

Eventually, the sobs lessened, and Link pulled back and wiped his eyes on the sleeve of his hoodie. He eyed Taeyang and winced. "Sorry, I made your shirt all wet."

"That is the absolute last thing I'm worried about." Taeyang sat back, rubbed his hand over Link's arm. "Are you all right?"

"There's been so much of everything," Link said, feeling

pathetic and weak. He laid his head back on the pillow and sighed, feeling a little lightheaded.

"I'm just gonna get you a drink," Taeyang said. "Some lemonade maybe, and then you can tell me everything."

In the few short moments while Taeyang was in the kitchen, Link tried to understand what had overwhelmed him just so much. He pulled the soft blanket closer around himself, loving the way it smelled of Taeyang and how warm it was.

Taeyang brought him a tall glass of lemonade and Link accepted it. "Thank you." He took a deep drink and sighed, it was exactly what he'd wanted. "I'm sorry, about uh, all of everything today."

Taeyang shook his head. "Stop apologizing, there's nothing to apologize for."

"I think there is," Link said. "I got really overwhelmed, because you were being so nice. And it's not that I don't want to be taken care of. It's because it brings back so much of… of how I was as a kid. My asthma was really bad back then, and Mom would, well, she was looking out for me. But there was all this stuff I couldn't do. I couldn't go to other kid's birthday parties, I missed a lot of school and every gym and swimming class. Our school had this big sports day, and I wasn't allowed… she was afraid I'd have an attack. Maybe I would have…" He swallowed and played with the corner of the blanket with one hand, trying to find the point he wanted to make with Taeyang.

Taeyang rubbed his knee over the blanket. "You don't have to tell me everything right now, if you don't want to."

A fresh wave of tears spilled out of Link's eyes. Taeyang was being so *nice*.

"Sorry, I didn't uh, mean to make things worse."

"You didn't. The thing is, when I was a kid I loved it, because it made me special and I knew Mom was doing it all because she loved me and she wanted me to be safe. But I hated it at the same time, I hated her keeping me back from things. Wrapping me up in cotton wool, even though I probably needed it."

"Sounds like you were pretty conflicted," Taeyang said,

haltingly. Link rubbed his eyes with the heel of his hand and sighed.

"Yeah, conflicted is right. And it messed me up. When I started to get better when I was a teenager, it eased off, I tried to be really independent instead. I did things for myself, and even when I was starting to get wheezy or feel tired, I'd just smile and act like things were okay, that I didn't need any help."

He sighed, thinking back on how he tried out for baseball against his mother's wishes. How he told everyone he was fine and sneaking a puff from the inhaler when people weren't looking. Taeyang moved closer, lifting Link's legs under the blanket so that he could slide in beside him, Link's legs over his lap. It was nice, closeness without being smothering. Link wasn't sure he could handle an arm around him just then. He picked up the lemonade and took a sip.

"Go on," Taeyang said.

"The thing was, I got so used to just… to pretending everything was all right, I guess. To not being a problem for anyone, that I guess I didn't know how to ask for help. I didn't know how to accept your help when you offered it. I felt like I had to stay out of your way or I'd be causing you problems, and then when you were nice to me, when you wanted to *take care of me*…" Link took a deep breath and let it out, enjoying how long he could exhale for now. How refreshing it felt. Taeyang's hand was on his knee, rubbing little circles. "It felt like I didn't deserve to be taken care of. Like I should push you away before it becomes a habit. I still feel like that, it's like, nervous butterflies in my stomach."

"I get that," Taeyang said. His voice low and soft. "I guess none of your previous partners ever really… took care of you?"

Link shook his head. "If I was sick or whatever, I just stayed away, told them not to come over. I was so afraid."

"Afraid of relying on it? Or them getting overbearing like you felt your mother had been?" Taeyang asked. He was being so *good and understanding*. Link felt another wave of tears spill over and swiped at his face with his sleeve again.

" No. Because with them and with you I was afraid because…

because what if I get used to you taking care of me and then you go away?" His voice broke on the last few words and he felt like a helpless child again. "None of this makes any sense, I know," he choked out.

Taeyang took the glass of lemonade off him, set it aside, and slowly, carefully, drew Link onto his lap to wrap him in his arms. "Is this okay?"

A moment before, Link would have said no, but that was before. He nodded and slipped his arm around Taeyang's shoulder. Taeyang held him tight.

"No one's asking for you to make sense right now, and in fact, human brains kind of… don't make sense. Our emotions can be fully irrational. I'm just so glad you told me," Taeyang said into Link's shoulder. "Now, let it all out."

Link buried his face in Taeyang's hair and sobbed. It took a few minutes, but then he started to get control of himself. It felt like he'd grieved for the scared child and rebellious teenager he'd been. He'd even let go of some of the resentment he felt towards his mother, and now he felt… washed clean? Emptier than he had before.

"Urgh, sorry, I just… uh, all over you," Link said.

Taeyang shook his head. "What did I say before about apologizing for crying on me?"

Link managed a smile. "I think you said there was nothing to apologize for."

"That's still true. Now, are you comfortable?"

Link nodded. He actually was, even though Taeayng's lap was a bit on the boney side, he felt warm and cared for and above all, safe.

"Shall we watch an episode of our show?" Taeyang asked. He reached for the remote. Link smiled at the idea that it was now 'our' show. But there was something else he wanted first. Being this close to Tae he couldn't resist asking.

"Yeah, just," Link wiped his face as best he could with his sleeve and then put his finger on Taeyang's chin. "Can I kiss you?"

"Uh, yeah. Yeah, you can." Taeyang's eyes met his, and they were so close. So near to kissing already, and his body was touching Link's in so many places that it felt like the most natural thing in the world.

Link leaned in and kissed Taeyang. It was even better than he'd imagined it would be. Tingles shot through him and he wanted nothing more than to keep on kissing Tae, perhaps forever.

Tae kissed back with a delicious certainty, a forcefulness that was intoxicating to Link. Tae's hand found its way into the hair at the back of Link's head and stroked and gently tugged, and Link moaned softly into Tae's mouth.

That sound seemed to somewhat break the spell and they both pulled back at the same time. Tae's eyes were hooded, half open and Link's mouth was dry again but this time it had nothing to do with asthma or medication.

"Okay, that was... really freaking amazing," Link said, not daring to talk louder than a murmur.

"Yeah, it was," Tae said. His eyebrows pulled together. "Okay, you need to get off my lap right now or I'm going to do some things that won't be considered restful for you."

"Don't threaten me with a good time," Link said, as he shuffled back onto the couch and pulled his legs up so Tae could get out from under him. He got to his feet a little unsteadily, which made Link feel inordinately pleased with himself.

"Soup and a show and then we can talk some more if you're up to it."

"Yes, boss," Link said, grinning happily.

A FEW HOURS LATER, TAEYANG WOKE UP. HE WAS ON THE COUCH, leaning against the armrest with Link snoring peacefully on his chest. They were both covered in the blanket and it was beginning to get uncomfortably warm.

But he couldn't bring himself to wake Link up. Rest was what Judy had said he needed, and he looked very relaxed. His cheek was on Taeyang's chest and his shoulder was pressed under Taeyang's arm. He could feel Link's arm around his waist, and what he could see of Link's face looked absolutely angelic and relaxed. Taeyang didn't want to disturb him for all the world.

Taeyang looked up at the TV, where Netflix had paused on the 'are you still watching?' check in screen. He wondered how long he'd been asleep so very carefully he pulled his hand out of the blanket, where it had been resting on Link's chest and checked his watch for the time. Almost five o'clock, they both must've been asleep for hours.

He breathed out, surprised, and winced when Link stirred. "Mm?"

"Nothing, go back to sleep," Taeyang said. He stroked Link's hair and Link made a happier version of the 'mm' noise, but his eyes were opening and his mouth curved in a self-satisfied smile.

"This is really nice," he said, sleepily. "But I need to pee."

He sat up, disentangling himself from Taeyang and

stretching, the blanket slid off his back and onto the floor. Taeyang watched him appreciatively, noting the strip of skin when his hoodie rode up and trying not to salivate or pounce on him.

He decided his legs needed stretching and got up as Link went to the bathroom. He carried their noodle bowls into the kitchen and rinsed them out. He gave in to a huge yawn. Taeyang couldn't remember the last time he'd had a nap like that in the middle of the day.

He must have needed it.

Link joined him in the kitchen a moment later, his hair adorably tousled and stifling another yawn. He came close in, like he was going to hug Taeyang or something but then stopped and took a step back.

"Uh, sorry, I guess I was just going to..." he cleared his throat.

"It's all right," Taeyang said. They hadn't kissed since that first time but the memory of it was fresh and vivid for Taeyang, he certainly wouldn't mind kissing Link again, but he guessed they needed to have another conversation before any more kissing happened.

"Thanks, again," Link said. For a moment Taeyang felt a horror that Link was thanking him for the kiss, but he kept speaking. "Letting me talk all that out and bawl on you and everything. I feel so much better now, lighter all round. I guess some of that had really been weighing on me."

"Of course," Taeyang said. He smiled. "Sometime I'll tell you about how weird it was moving away from home at age twelve to live in a country where hardly anyone speaks your native language."

Link winced in sympathy. "Yeah. I've got some questions about that for sure. But uh, first, where do we stand on the physical affection side of things?"

Taeyang felt like his whole body was smiling. "Uh, I'm not sure where we stand. My opinion on it is that it's good and I'd like to hug and kiss you again. But also I guess we should have another conversation about what we're doing?"

Link grinned and moved into Taeyang's personal space, went on his toes and kissed him on the lips.

He knew it'd be good. It had been good to kiss him earlier, had made him realize how long it had been since he'd kissed anyone at all, let alone someone he liked as much as he liked Link. But the kiss still outdid his expectations. His hands went to Link's waist and pulled him closer. He tilted his head and deepened the kiss as Link responded, winding his arms around him and moaning softly into his mouth.

When they broke the kiss, Link stayed close, his eyes starry in the kitchen light and so close. Taeyang pressed his forehead to Link's and smiled.

"I could get used to that," Taeyang said.

"Careful, Tae," Link said, a wicked smile lighting up his face even further. "What if we get too attached and it affects our performance in the park?"

It was meant as a joke, but it hit a little too closely to Taeyang's dream of Link and the Fairyland parade. He must have stiffened because Link looked at him quizzically. "You don't think it actually could affect our performance?"

Taeyang shrugged and huffed out a breath. "Well, I did have a dream that my feelings for you took over..."

"Oh, are you going to tell me the details now or do I have to guess?" Link pressed his hips against Taeyang's, which was extraordinarily distracting and did absolutely nothing for his train of thought.

"I was annoyed with you, and I wanted to show you that I was... uh, take control of you, perhaps is the better way to put it." He could feel warmth in his cheeks, and lower down, come to think of it, so he gently stepped backwards before the situation got more intense.

Link's eyes lit up. "Oh ho! You went full villain huh? I mean, I might not be averse to a little of that..."

Taeyang shook his head and laughed. "Not today, not when you had an asthma attack and need to rest, and both of us need-"

He gestured between the two of them. "Need to think things through."

Link nodded and leaned against the kitchen counter, his expression pure Fairy Mischief. "Well, I for one am a fan of doing rather than overthinking, but I take your point. I will insist on cuddles on the couch, but then I'll be good and go to bed and rest."

"Fantastic," Tae said. "What would you like for dinner?"

"More of the soup," Link said. He turned to sniff at the pot where it sat on the cold stove element. "It was awesome."

"All right. I think I have some frozen dumplings I can add to it as well, just for a little variety." Tae turned to the freezer, rummaged for a moment and produced packaged pork and chives dumplings from his favourite Asian grocer.

"I love you," Link said, his hands in his pockets and his expression open and hungry. Taeyang's heart fluttered but then he caught the exact direction of Link's gaze, it was on the packet of dumplings in his hand.

He lifted the packet above his head and Link's eyes followed it. Like a dog following a ball.

"You're ridiculous," he said, lowering his arm.

"Yeah, well," Link said. "You love that about me."

Taeyang's chest warmed and he smiled and said nothing at all.

CILLIAN TEXTED THE NEXT MORNING TO SAY HIS APARTMENT WOULD BE ready at the end of the week.

Link sat backstage, waiting for his cue for the first run through with an audience for the Fairyland villains show. He was a little nervous, so he'd been playing a match three game on his phone to distract himself. In costume, he sat on the folding chair, knees under his chin, and stared at the screen. He read Cillian's text three times.

The text was welcome news, but Link couldn't deny he also felt afraid. He didn't want to leave Taeyang's place. He enjoyed it there. He wanted to stay where Tae could take care of him.

But a bigger part of him knew that was a bad reason to stay. He had made it on his own this far, and sure, his car wouldn't start the last time he tried it, and he really needed to get that sorted out. He was still leaning on Taeyang for sensible food options and rides to work and back, but he had managed to save some money over the past couple of weeks.

He thumbed away from the chat app and opened his banking app, checking his balances. Not great, but not entirely dire. The full time Monday to Friday shifts had been good money. That was all about to change of course, the training only had a few days left and then their shifts would be all over the place again, four days on and three days off, shifts going into the evening and weekends… but that was all right. He didn't envy Arlo trying to schedule them all so they'd all be in at the same time to do the show twice a week.

Not my problem.

My problem is, as it always has been, me.

What do I want to do? I want to stay with Tae and try and make this work. Try and have a real relationship with him. But is that what's best for me? What's best for Tae?

Link sighed and set his phone down.

Tae was currently onstage with the other villains. He looked over towards Rosa, but he didn't want to bring her into this. Maybe he should see if Cillian was available for a talk later? Or… Lily Ysabel was close to Taeyang, maybe she'd have some insight?

Or… no.

I should just talk straight to Taeyang and express what I'm worried about. That's the adult thing to do. And further, I should wait until our shifts are over. No sense putting him off his game or disturbing him if I don't need to.

So, Link tried to put the dilemma out of his mind and concentrate on work. The show ended up being a lot of fun, the kids in the audience really reacted to the conflict and the drama and in the end when the good guys were triumphant there were cheers and applause.

They came off stage happy and smiling.

Link went to where his phone was, picked it up to check in on Cillian, flick him a message and see if they could hang out.

But there was a message Link didn't expect waiting for him.

Mom: Hey Lincoln, been a while since we heard from you. Tried your landline but it's been disconnected, getting a bit worried! Get in touch, sweetie xoxo Mom

Link frowned. Back at the old apartment they'd literally had a landline for one reason only: so their parents could get in touch with them. Link hadn't even considered it when he'd moved out, and he thought he'd told his mother he'd moved… but then again, maybe he didn't. He'd been so stressed he hadn't really been thinking straight.

He thumbed through the message history and no, he hadn't been in touch since before all the house moving drama. He hadn't had time, or rather, he hadn't had emotional energy to call his mother, and explain it all, and resist her inevitable invitation to come and stay. He hadn't been feeling nearly resilient enough, and he'd put it off and put it off. Now his mother was freaking out.

He'd better call her. But first he could get changed into his own clothes, at least. Get the gold glitter off his cheeks. The knowledge that he had to call sat in his stomach like a heavy stone.

"Ready to go?" Taeyang asked. He'd come up behind Link where he was sitting at the dressing table, changed and ready, but staring at his phone with dread.

"Uh, yeah, I just need to call my Mom, do you mind waiting? Or I could just wait and call when I get home, I guess."

"You can call her in the car," Taeyang suggested. Link shook his head.

"No, I'll do it now and get it over with," he said. "I want to enjoy the drive home if I can."

Taeyang nodded. "Okay, I might go grab a drink at the Forest Kitchen then. How about you meet me there when you're done?"

"Sure," Link managed a smile for Taeyang and watched him catch up with Phoenix James.

"Fifi, you want a hot cocoa?" Taeyang asked.

"Abso-LUTE-ly I do, Tae-Tae," Phoenix James said, slinging an arm over Taeyang's shoulders.

Link smiled a bit easier, watching the two of them and hearing their pet names. The others were leaving in dribs and drabs, and Nate paused by Link's chair to squeeze his shoulder.

"Great work out there today, Link."

"Yeah, you too," Link said. "Especially with that tree joke, the audience loved it."

"Thanks. Have a nice night." Nate grinned and was gone.

Link took a deep breath, picked up his phone and called his mother, Sandra. She picked up on the second ring.

"Link, oh my God, I thought you'd died in a ditch somewhere."

"Hey Mom. No, I'm all right." Link closed his eyes and tried to draw strength from the universe, but nothing much changed. His mother certainly hadn't changed.

"Well, thank goodness. Where have you been? What happened to your phone line?"

"Oh, well, I moved out of that place," Link said. "Roxy and Liam and everyone were finding new places and I couldn't afford it on my own so I moved out."

"Oh, how is Roxy?" Link sighed. Sandra really liked Roxy, and for some reason wanted Link and Roxy to be dating, even though Link had explained she was a lesbian a number of times. "That girl is so fashionable."

"Yeah, she's great, she's moved in with her long term girlfriend," Link said. He tried to put extra emphasis on the 'long term' part.

"So, what's your new place like?"

Link had forgotten that one of the things he found draining about talking to his mother was the whiplash of fast changing topics. He swallowed. "Well, I'm not exactly in the new place yet, I'm staying with a friend while Cillian moves out so I can take his place." *Theoretically. Unless I decide to stay with Tae. Unless Tae asks me to stay more like, I can't just decide to move into his spare room that would be so weird.*

"Oh." Sandra took a couple of seconds to think that through. "Which friend?"

"Well, he's a new friend, actually," Link said. He was infinitely glad that he had the changing room to himself, as the idea of describing Taeyang over the phone was mortifying. "His name's Taeyang and he was hired a couple of months back to play Lord Order at Fairyland."

"Taeyang, that's an unusual name," Sandra said. Link leaned forward until his forehead was resting on the workbench. He knew she was fishing for more information, about Taeyang's nationality, and he didn't want to give in to that.

But, he'd always given in to her before and force of habit won out.

"Yeah, he's from South Korea," Link said, his voice a little smaller. "Anyway I'm staying in his spare room."

"If you needed a spare room you could've used your old room here," Sandra said. "I could have had it ready for you in a moment's notice. In fact, you still could use it."

"I'm alright though," Link said. "I can stay with Tae, and it's a lot closer for work. We've been carpooling in."

"Hmm, well, I suppose that makes sense," she said, grudgingly. "But I miss you honey. Your sister's going to be down this weekend, why don't you pop around and come say hello?"

"Oh, Bianca's down? Uh, well, Cillian said the apartment would be free by then, so I should really be moving," Link said. But even as he said it he knew moving house wouldn't take him more than a couple of hours. It's not like he had couches and big pieces of furniture to move.

"Oh go on, I'll make a big supper for us all, it'll be nice. Have all the family together, we haven't done that in a very long time." Her tone was part wheedling, but also part confident that he'd give in and agree. And Link considered. It *was* a good opportunity to see his sister, and he hadn't had his mother's cooking for a long time. Maybe it would be nice.

"Ah, yeah, okay, sounds good. Saturday?"

"Yes, Saturday afternoon, turn up from three o'clock."

"Okay, sure," Link said. His voice had become smaller again and he cleared his throat, trying to will some confidence back into himself.

"Great, it's all settled then. No need to bring anything, love you, Lincoln. See you Saturday."

"Love you, see you," Link said, although Sandra hung up before he was all the way through the sentence. He sighed and stared at his phone. Then he remembered with a horrible sick feeling that his car had probably broken down.

He sighed, pocketed his phone and got up, making his way through the park to the Enchanted Forest Kitchen. The weather hadn't been as warm as before, so he zipped up his hoodie and squared his shoulders as he made his way through the park.

The Forest Kitchen was busy, but Link spotted Phoenix James and made his way over to their table.

"There he is, the number one most annoying fairy in all the land," Phoenix James said, laughing. Link forced a chuckle and sat down, sliding into the booth beside Taeyang.

"And proud of it. But I reckon you could be giving me a run for my money, Coldness," Link said.

"Lies and slander," Phoenix James said airily. "The fans adore me, haven't you seen? I'm literally blowing up on social media."

"If you were *literally* blowing up that would be a different thing," Link said. "Actually, I haven't really been online much. You're blowing up? That's awesome. Congrats." He meant it too, it was awesome that a new character could get traction so fast.

"Thank you." Phoenix James smiled and sipped their hot cocoa. "I shall have to send Max Jones a gift basket."

"I heard his taste is rather expensive," Taeyang said. He nudged a mug of frothy cocoa towards Link. "I got this one for you, I gambled on mint chocolate?"

"Oh, uh, thanks." Link hadn't expected that at all but it was a welcome surprise. He took the cup and wrapped both his hands around it, inhaling the smell and sighing happily.

"You're welcome." Taeyang leaned in and put his arm along the top of the booth back. It wasn't around Link, but it quite easily could have been.

For a moment, Link had forgotten about his mother and his promised visit, and he was very tempted to continue to forget, to put it out of his mind and deal with it later. But that tactic hadn't served him well lately, so he sighed and frowned at his cocoa and swallowed.

"Something you want to say?" Phoenix James said, with a hint of amusement.

"Just, uh, I said I'd go visit my folks this weekend, but also I'm meant to be moving and also also I'm pretty sure my car needs work." He cleared his throat and looked sideways at Taeyang. "Do you think I could borrow your car, please?"

Taeyang pulled his arm back and folded his hands on the table. Link felt a shiver as if a source of warmth had been removed. "You said they were a few hours away didn't you?"

"That's right," Link said.

"Well," Taeyang said, slowly. "What if I drove you? I actually love driving when I can get out of the city."

Link didn't think he could be surprised any more with how generous Taeyang was capable of being, but he was surprised all the same.

"Sounds like a fun getaway," Phoenix James said.

"Sure," Link said. "And if that's a nice way of saying you don't trust me with your nice car, I totally appreciate that you tried to hide it."

Taeyang nudged Link with his elbow, gently. "It's just that you're not on the insurance…"

Phoenix James and Link both laughed, but Link leaned in and gave Taeyang a peck on the cheek to say thank you.

THE WEEK FLEW BY, BETWEEN THE SHOWS AND A COUPLE OF MEET AND greets, plus evenings where Link filled up Taeyang's time. Link was naturally affectionate, so they'd soon progressed to cuddling on the couch while they watched TV in the evenings, and sometimes Link would thread his fingers through Taeyang's and that always sent pleasant tingles through him. But they hadn't really kissed again. A peck on the cheek here and there, but nothing as intense and passionate as the first time.

Taeyang wanted more, of course, but he still felt a little odd about their circumstances and Link being so unstable. Link also wasn't putting the moves on him, or indicating in any real way that he wanted to take things further, so Tae was happy to leave it at couch cuddles and the odd brief kiss.

It became a habit very quickly, and Taeyang started to wonder about how cold and empty the apartment would be once Link had moved out. He wondered, in fact, if Link had to move out at all, or if he could stay...

Saturday dawned and Taeyang got dressed in workout clothes. He was in the kitchen making a smoothie when Link stumbled in, still half asleep and yawning.

"Choo doin?" he mumbled. "Your pants... tight."

Taeyang glanced down at his workout leggings and chuckled.

"Uh, yeah, I was going to hit the gym so I can be washed and ready to go to your folks place whenever you want to leave."

Link groaned softly and pushed both hands through his hair. "I forgot."

"I'm... sorry?" Taeyang couldn't quite keep his amusement out of his voice.

"I wanna workout," Link said into the palms of his hands. Then he dropped his arms, and went back to his room, apparently without fully opening his eyes.

Taeyang turned back to the blender, half expecting he'd hear snores from behind the closed door.

But Link resurfaced a couple of minutes later in his workout gear, and they headed to the gym together.

In the mid-afternoon they were dressed more formally. Link had traded his usual Fairyland branded T-shirt and hoodie for a heather blue button down that brought out his eyes in a very fetching way, and dark indigo jeans with no holes in them. Taeyang had opted for black chinos and a pristine white T-shirt under a black and white bomber jacket with a cherry tree embroidered on the back of it.

"You look good," Link said. He sucked on his lower lip as he looked Taeyang up and down, nodding appreciatively. "Um, Mom's going to think you're my boyfriend."

"You did tell her I was coming, didn't you?"

"Yeah, of course. But like, I don't normally bring anyone, so it'll... she'll read into it."

Taeyang's skin felt prickly and he fidgeted with his car keys. "I guess we haven't really had the talk about what we're doing or what we call... us," he said.

The silence stretched between them and Link was chewing on his lower lip and looking lost, so Taeyang said the first thing that came into his head.

"Do you *want* to introduce me as your boyfriend? I mean, you can just say friend, it's fine."

Link moved a little closer and reached up to touch Taeyang's cheek very softly with the tip of his fingers. "I don't want to say you're just my friend, Tae."

Taeyang's breath caught and he searched Link's eyes for any trace of a joke or trick, but there was nothing there. Link wasn't, after all, actually Fairy Mischief. He was Lincoln, and maybe he didn't exactly have everything together in his life, but he wouldn't joke about something as important as this. Taeyang was certain of that.

"Well, then," Taeyang said. "Are you my boyfriend?"

Link's grin was instant and infectious, and Taeyang was smiling when Link kissed him. "Yeah," he said against Taeyang's lips.

Taeyang's heart did a triple beat of happiness and he pulled Link closer by the loops on his jeans, kissing him harder so he had to tip his head back.

It feels so good, so right. Not like kissing anyone else. Nothing has ever felt as right as this does.

Link made a deliciously needy noise and for a moment Taeyang forgot he was okay with taking things slow, and that Link hadn't been pushing for more. He forgot, well, everything except for the taste of Link's toothpaste and some kind of flavored lip balm he'd used and how much Taeyang wanted to push him against the wall and take him apart.

Kiss his skin, kiss up his neck, bite a little perhaps, see how he likes that...

But Link pulled back from the kiss and exhaled hard through his nose. "Um, we should... I mean, I really want to just give in to you right now and follow you to bed and do absolutely everything we can think of but... my folks are expecting us." He looked down, possibly more disappointed than Taeyang was.

"No, right, of course you're right," Taeyang said. He swallowed and let go of Link's waist. His hands had moved, all on their own, to Link's lower back, and then one was under the hem of his shirt. He swallowed down the sudden lust that had risen in him and smiled.

Link managed a smile back but from the rapid movement of his chest Taeyang could see he'd had an effect on him as well.

"Breathing okay?" Taeyang asked. "Don't need your inhaler?"

Link shook his head. "This has nothing to do with asthma. I'm breathing fine, but thanks for checking."

"Of course." Taeyang spun the keys in his hand and turned to go out the door, pausing when Link spoke again.

"But, I might bring it just in case. The weather's sometimes cooler in San Diego."

The drive to Link's parent's house was remarkably pleasant. The highway was busy but not jammed with traffic, and the view over the Pacific Ocean was stunning. It wasn't a drive Taeyang had done before and he appreciated it, remarking out loud every now and then to Link.

Link on the other hand, got quieter and quieter as the drive went on. Taeyang glanced at him as the GPS navigation told him his exit, and saw he was sitting lower in his seat, his expression serious.

"Hey, it's okay," Taeyang said. "If you want to leave early make a signal and I'll invent something, like a text from an auntie or something."

Link looked over at him, startled as if he'd forgotten that Taeyang was there in the car with him.

"Huh? Oh, it's okay, I'll be fine once I get there," he said. Taeyang liked how quickly Link understood his meaning. "It's just the anticipation that gets me."

"I get that," Taeyang said. He hadn't been back to Korea in four years but the thought of it made his stomach a little queasy. And he loved his parents, and he loved Korea, so there really wasn't a reason why it should feel that way.

Well, no reason beyond *family*.

Taeyang followed the GPS instructions and pulled up in front of a cute, well maintained two storey bungalow with a wraparound verandah. The lawns were bright green and perfectly maintained, and there was a selection of plaster figures dotted into the flowerbeds. Taeyang thought one of them might be a Treasure the Unicorn.

Link took a deep breath and looked uncertainly at Taeyang. "Thanks for coming with me, and I am sincerely sorry for what's about to happen."

Taeyang snagged Link's hand in his and squeezed it, getting the feeling he shouldn't kiss him just now, in front of his parent's house. Link squeezed his hand back and exhaled noisily. "Whatever happens, I have your back. And remember, the auntie excuse is always there."

Link smiled. "We didn't establish a signal."

"Whatever makes sense in the moment," Taeyang said. He smiled again, hoping he was being encouraging to this strange, mercurial but endearing man. Link smiled at him but his eyes still looked a little frightened.

"Right, well," Link said. "May as well get it over with." He got out of the car with a distinct air of trepidation. Tae followed him up the pristine path to the home of Sandra and Owen Miller.

Link didn't bother with ringing the doorbell, he just opened the door and walked in, calling out as he stepped inside. "Hello!"

"In here," a male voice responded. Taeyang left his shoes by the door, even though Link hadn't bothered. It was a lifetime habit he couldn't just choose to ignore. He padded after Link into a den where Sandra and Owen stood. The family resemblance was clear - Link had his father's sandy, strawberry blond hair and his mother's sparkling eyes. Her nose and his jawline. They were hugging him hello and smiling warmly.

"Mom, Dad," Link said, pulling back and gesturing towards Taeyang. "This is Taeyang, he's my maybe boyfriend."

Sandra's smile faded in radiance to something more polite and practised. "Oh, hello, Taeyang." Her eyes flicked up and down his body and Taeyang felt judged.

"It's nice to meet you," Taeyang said. He walked forward to shake Owen's proffered hand.

"Oh my GOD! Is that Linkie?!" A younger female voice came

from behind him, accompanied by a thundering of steps down the stairs. Taeyang had barely turned to look when a woman with long dark hair enclosed Link in a huge hug. He laughed, picked her up and spun her around.

"Binkie!" he cried out.

This had to be Link's sister, and Taeyang realized he hadn't ever heard her name. Link set her down and grinned at Taeyang. "This is my sister, Bianca. Binkie, this is Taeyang, he's my kind of boyfriend."

"What's a kind of boyfriend?" Bianca asked, giggling a little. She reached out to shake Taeyang's hand. "Nice to meet you, Taeyang."

"Nice to meet you, too," Taeyang said.

"What are we all standing around for?" Owen said. "Come on through to the dining room, let's sit down."

"Dinner is almost ready, very close," Sandra said. "Oh I hope you're not a vegetarian, Taeyang?"

Taeyang shook his head. "No, I'll eat most things."

"Good man," Owen said, nodding appreciatively. Taeyang thought it was a strange thing to be approving of, but at least he had a little approval from Link's dad.

"Come on through."

They all moved through into the dining room and Owen sat at the head of the table. Link sat to his left and Bianca went around the table to sit on his right. Taeyang went to sit beside Link, where there was a table setting. The other one, opposite him, must have been where Sandra was going to sit.

"So, how was the drive?" Owen said.

Link looked at Taeyang before answering. "Oh, it was pretty fine. Not too much traffic."

"No, it was pretty smooth," Taeyang said.

"I can't believe you're dating the guy who's playing Lord Order," Bianca said. She eyed Taeyang and grinned. "I mean, that photo of you carrying Link out like he's a swooning princess was absolutely incredible though."

Sandra walked in with a huge platter of fried chicken and set it down in the middle of the table. "What? Why were you carrying Link? Was it a part of a show?"

"No," Link said. His answer clipped. He cleared his throat. "This chicken looks great, Mom."

"Thanks," she said, automatically. "Link, if it wasn't part of a show why was he carrying you?"

Taeyang bit his tongue and tried to think of a way to change the topic of conversation, since Link clearly didn't want to talk about it. "Do you need a hand getting anything else out of the kitchen, Mrs Miller?"

Sandra shook her head, apparently she wouldn't be distracted by anyone. "Lincoln, you tell me what happened."

"I uh," Link seemed to deflate, his shoulders slumping. "I had a slight asthma attack in the park, the temperature dropped really suddenly and I guess it got to my chest." He spoke as if he were an ashamed schoolkid, being caught doing something he knew he shouldn't have. Taeyang felt outrage bubbling in his chest on his behalf.

"You what?" In an instant Sandra was beside Link, her hand on his shoulder. "Oh, my poor baby, I can't believe it's all come back after all this time."

"It hasn't *all come back*," Link said, with fierce emphasis. "I just had one attack out of nowhere, and it was fine. The Fairyland staff had an inhaler I could use and it passed."

Sandra tutted her tongue against her teeth. "It starts with just one attack, and then it progresses. Have you been taking care of yourself?"

"Yeah," Link said. "Of course I have," but his eyes flashed to Taeyang.

As if he's feeling guilty. Oh, because he was so stressed about moving house, he wasn't sleeping and hardly eating. It'd put a strain on his body, made him weaker… but I won't say anything about that. No sense in worrying Sandra even more than she already is.

"Maybe you should stay the night instead of driving home after dark," Sandra said. She put her hand on Link's forehead.

Astounded, Taeyang looked to Owen and Bianca, but neither of them had reacted to Sandra's fussing. *They must be used to this.*

"That's really not necessary," Link said. "Taeyang's car is nice and warm, I'll be fine."

"Hmm." Sandra dropped her hand and shook her head. "I don't like it, Lincoln. Not one bit. I remember how sick you were back then, and how it made you so weak."

Owen sighed. "Just leave the boy," he said. "Come on, we're smelling this chicken but we can't eat any until everyone's sitting down."

"Oh, of course," Sandra flapped her hands. "Start serving yourselves, I'll get the other dishes out."

"Would you like a hand carrying things?" Taeyang asked. He started to get up from his chair but Sandra gestured downwards.

"No, I've got it." She hurried into the kitchen and Owen picked up the tongs and served himself two pieces of chicken before passing the tongs to Link. Link took a piece and handed the tongs to Taeyang.

Taeyang was giving himself his second piece when Sandra returned with a large bowl of mashed potatoes and a jug of gravy, which she set down and then immediately turned back to go into the kitchen.

Taeyang gave the tongs to Bianca who smiled politely at him and then leaned forward to hiss at Link. "I'm sorry Linkie, I didn't mean to start a whole thing…"

Link scrunched his nose up and shrugged. "It's fine."

Sandra returned with a large pan of green beans and finally took her seat beside Bianca. Taeyang looked down at his plate and tried hard not to feel resentful of Sandra. He reminded himself that she was fussing over Link because she cared about him and she was afraid.

35 / LINK

Dinner was delicious, Link knew this logically. He'd eaten his mother's fried chicken before and he knew it was delicious. But tonight he could barely taste anything. He ate, although he didn't feel hungry at all, he ate because if he didn't people, his mother, would notice, and say something. He didn't want more attention on him. He chewed and swallowed, but his stomach was a knot of tension, and his mouth felt dry.

He barely heard the conversation, although he knew it was going on. He heard the voices as if from far away. His father and sister talking about what Bianca had been up to in her job. Her job which, Link mused, had never been very clear to him. It was something to do with making teams of people work more efficiently. She was a consultant so she worked at lots of different companies and offices, there was always a lot of ground to cover there, conversationally speaking.

At one point, as Link was gazing at her and trying to imagine what she would be like in a formal, professional setting, she caught his eye and gave a slight nod.

It took him a few minutes to decipher but he thought it meant she knew she was drawing attention away from him. That she was doing it on purpose.

He loved her very much in that moment.

Link took the time to be quiet and unnoticed as he ate, trying to calm down his stomach as he swallowed each bite.

He realized, after a while longer, as everyone was finishing up their chicken and sides, and Sandra started to make noises about dessert, that no one had asked Taeyang anything.

No one had asked about his family, or what he did at Fairyland.

No one had asked Link about his job, either, but at least they knew what Link did, he'd talked about it before. The only thing they knew about Taeyang was that he was working with Link, and Bianca had seen a photo.

No one had asked Taeyang about him at all, really.

That bugged him, almost enough to distract him from his tense stomach and growing sense that he needed to flee, even though he couldn't just flee.

Couldn't they see how awesome Taeyang was? How much he cared and thought about others? How handsome he was? Surely they should be asking him all sorts of things to get to know him. But instead, no, just endless anecdotes from Bianca about people and companies Link had never heard of.

But that was unfair, she was directing attention away to protect Link, wasn't she?

Link looked down at the dregs of mashed potatoes on his plate and tried to get his mind to think just one thought at a time.

Why don't they care about Tae though? I introduced him as my maybe boyfriend, that's kind of a big deal. It's been ages since I brought anyone home at all.

Maybe I shouldn't have said maybe boyfriend, it kind of lessened the impact of how much he means to me, but like, we're so new, and I couldn't just call him my boyfriend straight out like we've been dating for months.

I hope he's not bored out of his mind listening to all this talk about Bianca's job.

He looked at his mother and tried to decipher her. It wasn't the first time, and it almost certainly wouldn't be the last time either.

She was so many contradictions. Loving and kind, but no

nonsense and impossible to argue with. She would never say she was wrong, never. It was stubbornness, Link supposed, and he also supposed he had inherited some of that.

His aversion to conflict was certainly a result of her iron will, and her refusal to compromise. Why even try to argue if you knew you would never win? Far easier to bend and agree, let her have the moment.

But she had cared for him when he was sick… he could never forget that. His father visited him in hospital but only seldomly, bringing teenaged Bianca along, rolling her eyes and focusing on her phone. His mother would spend hours at his bedside, reading to him or telling him what she could see outside the window when he was too weak to look himself.

That was love.

But he didn't need that now. Or if he did, he wanted to choose Taeyang to do it for him.

Then he remembered with a jolt, the time he'd gone into an appointment as a twelve year old, his mother beside him. *His doctor smiling.*

"You know, asthma treatment's really come along in the last few years, we understand it a lot better. With the right combination of preventer and relievers, there's no reason Lincoln can't try out for sports if he feels up to it. In fact, some exercise could be very beneficial."

Sandra had smiled and nodded, and as soon as they'd left, she'd found Link a different doctor. "I'd just be more comfortable if you didn't exert yourself needlessly, that's all," she'd said.

"LISTEN, LINKIE, MAYBE YOU OUGHT TO STAY THE NIGHT, JUST SO THAT your chest stays warm," Sandra said. She said it carelessly, as if she'd only just then thought of it. The family had moved into the living room and were on the couches, with cups of tea and coffee and to Taeyang it felt as if she'd been carefully planning her moment to spring this suggestion on him. Waited until he was relaxed and off guard.

"Oh, uh…" Link's smile was plastic and as fake as anything Taeyang had ever seen from him. He was beside Taeyang on the couch, so Taeyang was close enough to see the muscle jumping in his jaw. "Yeah, I guess that would be fine."

"There's really no need," Taeyang said, quickly. "Besides, I'm driving, how would he get home in the morning?"

Link blinked and looked at Taeyang, as if he were just waking up.

"I'm just a bit worried," Sandra said. "He's very frail, you know, and it does get cold once the sun goes down."

"He's not frail actually," Taeyang said. He felt his anger pushing words to the surface and his annoyance with Sandra trumped his desire to be polite.

That, and he hated the effect she had on Link. This wasn't the Link he knew and cared for. This was someone who had been gently bullied into submission and agreement over the years, and Taeyang wanted his Link back.

My Link? Okay, I guess that's how I'm feeling about him.

"I'm sorry, I don't think I quite caught that," Sandra said.

"Link is a grown man, he's fit and strong. He's great at his job, which by the way is largely outdoors and very physically demanding, and you're calling him frail because he had a single asthma attack a week ago?"

Link looked shaken, he'd gone pale and his eyes were wide. Taeyang glanced at him and saw he was shaking his head ever so slightly.

"Tae, uh, thanks but maybe just cool it a little, it's fine. I really was sick as a kid, and she's-"

"Young man, I won't have you talk to my wife like that," Owen barrelled in straight over what Link had said.

Taeyang looked around the living room. Sandra was pink in the face, her knuckles white where she held her mug of coffee. Owen had set his cup down but otherwise hadn't moved, sitting rigid in the armchair and watching Taeyang sharply. Bianca, seated on the other couch beside her mother, had a peculiar expression, eyebrows raised and her mouth twitching. Was she enjoying this?

"It's fine," Link said, again. His voice reedy and strange as he tried to keep the peace. "Mom had to go through so much back then. All that time in the ER, not sure if I was going to die, all the bills, everything, I was a huge burden."

"*You* were the one sick, you went through it as well. Perhaps even more than she did," Taeyang said. He wasn't sure if Link really believed what he was saying, the tone of his voice indicated he didn't - but he was stalwartly defending his mother despite looking like he wanted to bolt from the room.

"Not that we, honey we didn't think of you as a *burden*," Sandra said. Her smile had returned, and it was sickly sweet. "The money didn't matter at all, we just wanted you to be well. Our brave little boy." She looked put upon and sad, but in a sort of noble, self-sacrificing sort of way.

Taeyang noticed that she hadn't addressed his point about Link being the one who'd actually been sick. No doubt she had suffered, worrying about him, but surely she should be glad he'd got well enough to have a proper life now?

Taeyang understood, better than ever, why Link hadn't wanted to come and stay with his folks when he'd had no luck with an apartment. He flashed back to the conversation they'd had in Taeyang's apartment. Link had said *"I hated her keeping me back from things. Wrapping me up in cotton wool, even though I probably needed it."*

She'd been protecting him, perhaps when he didn't need it, and he'd been so fiercely trying to prove himself and that he was independent. He had been sick, but he wasn't right now, and Taeyang wouldn't let him fall back into old, bad routines with his mother.

"He's not a little boy now."

"We worry about him as if he was one," Owen said.

"Maybe, instead of worrying about him, you could back off and let him live his life," Taeayng said. "If he needs your help, if he wants it, he'll come to you then."

Link put his hand on Taeyang's arm. "It's fine, Tae," Link said, his voice hushed.

"It's not fine!" Taeyang's voice was louder than he'd meant it to be and everyone in the room seemed to sit back slightly. "You weren't… you were sick but you didn't need to be wrapped in cotton wool, that's what you told me."

Link blinked and seemed to be seeing Taeyang clearly for the first time in a few minutes. "Right."

"And yeah, you had an attack a week ago but you rested and you've been good since," Taeyang felt his mind veer away from saying the word 'fine', it seemed to be loaded with meaning in his house. "We came for dinner, we've had dinner, and it was lovely, but I'm beginning to think we ought to go."

Bianca stood up abruptly and smiled. "I think that's a great idea, honestly," she said. It was the first time she'd spoken in a while and Taeyang searched her face for what it could mean. Was she angry with Taeyang as well? He didn't think so, her eyes crinkled around the corners and she gave Taeyang a quick wink.

Link stood up next, setting his cup down on the side table and then clapping his hands together once. "Yeah, uh, thanks for a great dinner Mom, it was good to see you Dad, but we really should be hitting the road, long drive home and all."

He sounded more like himself, which gave Taeyang some hope. Taeyang stood up too.

"Now, just a minute, you can't come in here and make a scene and expect-" Owen started. Bianca cut him off.

"It was just lovely to meet you, Taeyang," she said. She took him by the elbow and led him out of the living room and towards the front door, Link close behind them. Once they were in the hallway she dropped her bright tone. "Seriously, you rock. Thanks for saying all that, back there."

"Oh, I… what?" Taeyang was still struggling to catch up with what was happening.

"Link and Mom have been in this pattern for a long time," she said. "And I had no idea how to help. Helping him get into gymnastics as a teenager kinda helped, I used to drive him to practice, but…" she shook her head. "It's like they always go back to the same script."

Link opened the front door, obviously eager to make his escape as quickly as possible, but he hesitated for a moment to smile at his sister. "I didn't even realize…" he said. What he didn't realize wasn't spoken and apparently didn't need to be. Bianca let go of Taeyang and wrapped her brother in a warm hug, squeezing him.

"Maybe don't come back for a little bit," she said. "I'm leaving tomorrow, but I'll talk to them both. I think this guy, Tae? Is really good, you should probably make him into a definitely boyfriend, okay, Linkie?"

He squeezed her and kissed her cheek. "Thanks, Binkie. I love you."

"Love you too, call me okay? Thanks for all of this Tae, you're awesome, I'm a big fan." She all but pushed them both out the door. "And drive safe!"

37 /LINK

Once he was down the steps, and safely out of the house, Link looked back to wave at Bianca and blow her a kiss. The curtains to the living room were drawn and he couldn't see his parents. It was probably best that way. He took Taeyang's hand and squeezed it, but didn't manage any words until they were both in the car, and the car had left his parent's street.

"You're incredible."

Taeyang glanced at him and then back at the road. "You're not angry with me?"

"Why would I be angry with you? You're an avenging angel who came to my rescue. If you hadn't been there, I'd be making up my bed and staring at my old posters of Leonardo DiCaprio," Link said. It was sort of a joke, but it also really wasn't. He would have capitulated and stayed over, and Sandra would have driven him home the next day, but probably not until the afternoon, monopolizing his time and stretching things out.

"I'm sorry I spoke to your parents that way," Taeyang said. "It was rude of me."

"I dunno." Link stretched his legs out as far as they'd go in the footwell of the car and groaned as his knees made a soft popping noise. "I think they needed to hear it. Besides, they didn't ask a thing about you or your family or anything, and I reckon that's much ruder."

Taeyang sighed a little. "No, they didn't."

"I love you," Link said, surprising both of them. Even though he'd said it before, this time it just burst out of him.

Taeyang smiled softly, pulled the car off the road and turned off the ignition. "Yeah? You really mean that? You're not just... I dunno, riding high on adrenaline and feeling relieved that you're not staring at old Leo posters?"

Link half turned in his seat and took one of Taeyang's hands. He wanted him to believe this so badly, and he didn't know exactly how to make it sound sincere. But he had to try.

"Yeah, man. You're... you're so good. You're kind, and clever and handsome and... you're so much. I love all of it. Even your weird Instagram about lying things down together in a perfect pattern."

Taeyang chuckled. "I haven't done any knolling in a while."

"It's besides the point," Link said. He leaned his head against the headrest and gazed into Taeyang's eyes. "My point is that I love you, and I've loved living with you and I want to keep on doing that and I want to kiss and I want you to be my for real boyfriend."

Taeyang leaned closer and kissed Link softly on the mouth. "I love you too, Link. And I'd very much like to be your real boyfriend." Link's safety belt was cutting into his shoulder, so he unclipped it and shifted as close as he could to Taeyang, cursing the handbrake for getting in the way.

Tae's eyes were bright even in the dim light from the street and he was smiling, a soft, warm smile quite unlike anything Link had seen on his face before. He looked so beautiful, strong, sure of himself... a protector, but a partner too.

Taeyang cupped his cheek in one hand and for a moment they both just gazed at each other, breathing in time.

"Tae," Link said, finally, his voice small. He felt a wave of fear wash over him with what he was about to ask, but he didn't let it drown him. He knew Tae, and he trusted him. He asked anyway. "Will you please take me home and look after me?"

"Of course I will," Tae said. He kissed him again, then sat back in his seat, checked his safety belt and drove them home. Link leaned his head against the window and watched him as he drove, flushed with pleasure that Tae loved him back, and wanted to look after him and that now, Link could call Tae his.

THE NEXT DAY WAS SUNDAY, AND TAEYANG WOKE UP WARM AND happy, with a slumbering Link wrapped around him. They had agreed to not do anything more than kiss the night before, as emotions were raw, and things were still a bit new, but Link had come to bed with him.

He hadn't exactly expected to wake up as the little spoon though. It felt delightful, if new. With his previous partners Taeyang had generally been the big spoon, this was... it made him feel so precious somehow. He turned his head to nuzzle into Link's bicep where it cushioned his cheek. He smelled so good, like fresh grass and rain and a trace of sweat.

Taeyang brought his hand up to place it over Link's where it rested on his chest and sighed, enjoying the bliss this simple gesture brought him.

Knowing Link as he did, he knew he wouldn't wake up easily, so after a few more minutes of enjoying Link holding him, he tried to make his escape. He lifted Link's arm off his chest and made to shuffle towards the end of the bed. Link made a grumpy noise and pulled him closer in, wrapping his arms more firmly around him. Taeyang chuckled.

"Oh that's how it is, is it?" he said, aloud. Not particularly expecting a response.

"Stay," Link murmured into the hair at the back of his neck.

Taeyang melted, all intention to get up gone in an instant. He relaxed back against Link and smiled.

"If you insist."

"Mmhm." Link nuzzled the back of his neck and then kissed the skin there, sending hot tingles down the length of Tae's spine. If too much more of this happened, things were going to progress quickly, and Taeyang still thought they needed to talk. To have The Relationship Talk.

Link mouthed at the back of his neck seemingly randomly and Taeyang inhaled, trying to get a hold of himself. "Link," he said, his voice hoarse. "There's things we need to work out, before… before we do all that."

Link huffed against his neck and loosened his grip on Taeyang. "But you're so sexy," he whined. He was more awake than Taeyang had expected from him.

Taeyang's resolve wavered, but once they'd talked things through they could have all the lingering in bed that they wanted, with no uncertainty. He just had to be strong this once… He cleared his throat.

"Come on, get up now and I'll make pancakes and we can talk," he said. "And then come back to bed."

Link's grip on him tightened. "Pancakes?"

"Yeah."

"Okay, fine." Link kissed the back of his neck again and let go. Taeyang was truly sorry for it, and missed his warmth right away, but it was for the best.

Taeyang was cooking pancakes and Link was sitting at the table, yawning. He'd already set the table with plates, cutlery, maple syrup and glasses of orange juice and now his energy seemed to have run out. Taeyang brought the stack of pancakes to the table and sat opposite Link. They both helped themselves.

"Mmmm, this smells incredible," Link said, pouring maple syrup liberally over his breakfast and picking up his fork. "Thanks, Tae."

"You're welcome," Taeyang said. He watched Link eating, and wondered if it was normal to find something like that quite as adorable as he did, but there was nothing for it. He just loved Link, no matter what he did.

"So, you wanted to talk boundaries and stuff, I guess?" Link said, once he'd swallowed his mouthful.

"Uh, yeah," Taeyang said. "I mean, I just think we have some issues that might work against us if we're not careful. I mean, I've been pretty independent for a long time, and the last time I had a roommate was... well, years ago. I'm not saying I don't want you moving in permanently," he said quickly, interpreting a look of panic on Link's face. "Because I do want you to, but I might need some alone time and I might get cranky that you're in my space at certain times."

Link nodded. "That's fine, I like going out and spending time with Cillian or going to the gym, or whatever, so that's all good. Just let me know as early as you can, I'd rather not make you crabby if I can go out before it's a thing."

Taeyang smiled. "So, you're staying?"

Link took a breath and looked at his pancakes, hesitating before he replied. The hesitation set Taeyang's heart racing.

"Yeah, I want to stay," he said, slowly. "It's just, well, you saw how things were last night. I don't want you to have to baby me, I've tried so hard since I was a kid to be independent, and I think I was doing it in a shitty man-child way. I want to be a proper adult, so uh, if you don't mind reminding me of that if I start falling back on my old habits? Is that too much to ask?"

Taeyang smiled and shook his head. "No, that sounds really good."

Link smiled and took a quick drink of orange juice. "I think we've both been kind of doing some of this stuff already. Like, talking through things that worry us and being up front about our feelings."

"I think so, too," Taeyang said. He ate some of his breakfast and chewed thoughtfully. "What I'm really excited about though," he said, after a while. "Is that we can be each other's family."

Link's eyes widened and a slow smile lit his face up. "Oh, wow. I mean, I love my family and I will definitely want to go see them again, maybe not any time soon, but... that's such a great thought. Yes, let's do that."

Taeyang grinned and took Link's hand, squeezing it. This felt good, this felt right. All the worry in his stomach had gone and the day was looking bright.

"So, uh," Link grinned and looked at the diminished pile of pancakes. "You said that after we talked we could go back to bed."

"I did, yeah." Taeyang brought Link's hand to his mouth and kissed his knuckles.

"Have we talked through all the things?" Link asked. His eyebrows raised and he smiled hopefully.

"Mm. I think we have for now," Taeyang said. He got up and tugged Link to his feet, pulling him close against him and feeling his own breath quicken.

"Cool," Link said, his voice dreamy. He kissed Taeyang on the lips, a deep, intense kiss that didn't last nearly long enough before he pulled back and grinned, all mischief and promise. "Pretty sure it's this way…"

It had been more than a week since the disastrous family dinner. Link had unpacked all his boxes and settled into the spare room. Which was now properly his room. And although he slept most nights in Taeyang's bed with him, some nights he liked some space to himself. Well, to himself and his Spring the Rabbit plushie. Tae must have noticed the cuddly toy by now, but he hadn't commented on it at all, which Link loved about him.

On Monday morning his alarm went off and he found himself sprawled in the middle of the bed, drooling on the pillow. With a huge effort he hauled himself out of bed and into the nearest clean clothes. He found Tae in the kitchen, making a green smoothie and looking like a model. Link slipped one hand around Tae's waist and kissed him on the cheek.

"Good morning, zombie Link," Tae said. "Do you want one of these?"

Link tried to say no but it came out as more of a grunt than a word. He rested his head on Tae's shoulder. Maybe he could get just a little more sleep...

He had just dropped off when Tae moved, shaking him awake. "Come on, there's pop-tarts for you in the toaster."

"Mm. Thanks." Link made his way to the toaster and finally pried his eyes all the way open. He retrieved the pastries and made the trek to the kitchen table and sat opposite Tae, slowly waking up as he took in how cute and fresh his boyfriend looked in the morning light. The fact that he was his boyfriend was a constant delight as well.

"So, today I have some villain group appearances scheduled," Tae said. "The newbie villain cabal will be plotting your downfall." He grinned and took a slurp of his smoothie.

"My downfall?" Link asked. He took a bite of his pop-tart. "Mine in particular?"

"Oh yes,' Tae nodded. "We already figured out how to take down Valor and Patience, so…"

"Mm. Have fun," Link said. "For my part, I hope it involves lots of naked Lord Order and maybe some biting."

Tae grinned. "Maybe it will. Maybe Fairy Mischief needs to be spanked as well, it might put him in his place…"

"Okay," Link said, shifting in his seat. "This breakfast talk is getting very bedroomy."

Tae rubbed his foot along Link's leg and chuckled. "I'm just making sure you're awake." He dropped his foot to the floor and sat back. "So, you'll be running around and improvising today, I assume?"

Link took a deep breath and quelled his arousal. *Work, yes, focus on work.* "Yeah, just like in the old days."

It felt good, knowing he was still able to move freely in the forest and surprise people. His shifts were varied. Arlo was still working on the perfect schedule and mix of shifts, appearances and shows, but Link had been enjoying himself in the meantime. There were two shows this week, a parade on Saturday, some park appearances with Tae and some on his own.

By mid morning he was out in the Enchanted Forest, feeling full of energy and good humor. It had been a relatively quiet morning in the park, so he was delighted to recognize some familiar faces.

Freddie and his three daughters were making their way up the path towards him, but didn't appear to have seen him yet. Stella, the middle child, was wearing a black hoodie with the words

'Lord Order' spelled out on it in purple glitter. Must be from the brand new merchandise line, Link made a mental note to grab himself one at the end of the shift.

But for now… they hadn't seen him, so he gestured for Francisco to follow him, and half concealed himself behind a tree on the side of the path. Francisco huffed, and rolled his eyes, but he moved behind a nearby tree all the same to help with the surprise.

Link waited until they were a couple of yards away and let out his signature Fairy Mischief giggle.

"Mischief?" Jemima said, confused. She looked all around. It was Navi who spotted him.

"There!"

Link leapt out onto the path in front of them. "Surprise!"

The girls laughed and Freddie, dressed today in torn jeans, a heavy leather jacket and a red bandanna laughed loudest of all, clapping his hands.

"Fairy Mischief!" Navi ran at him and Link quickly sank to one knee so he could catch her in a hug. "I missed you!"

"Aw, I missed you, too," Link said.

"We were worried! You got sick and then Lord Order kidnapped you!" Stella said.

"Navi has been asking about you," Freddie said. After a squeezy hug, Navi let go and Stella darted in to give him a hug as well. Freddie smiled, and continued talking. "We couldn't come in all last week so we've been making up stories about what might have happened, haven't we, girls?"

"Yeah," Jemima said. She sidled closer and gave Link a quick one armed hug before moving back a bit, blushing slightly.

"Here's mine, it's for you Fairy Mischief." Navi pulled a crumpled envelope out of her pocket and thrust it towards Link.

"That's incredible, thank you so much," Link said. "But I'm completely okay now. Lord Order actually helped me, he didn't kidnap me. I'm not sure why, but maybe he was afraid of what his life would be like without a little mischief in it. He does like routines, after all and my making mischief is part of his routine." This was the agreed on storyline should anyone ask about the incident, or the photos of Tae carrying Link out of the park. Much nicer and less scary than Lord Order kidnapping him.

Freddie chuckled and Stella scrunched up her nose. "I bet it was really part of a bigger plan," she sniffed.

"Hm." Link stood up and folded his arms. "I did notice, Stella, that you appear to be wearing his livery."

"What's livery?" Navi asked.

"A costume or uniform that shows who you support or serve." Link said. "Are you on his side now?"

The sisters laughed and Stella put her hands on her hips. "Maybe I am. Wouldn't you like to know?"

"Come on, girls," Freddie said, waving his phone. "If you want a picture you'd better get it now. There's other people who want to talk to Fairy Mischief after all."

They posed together for a photo and Navi squeezed Link's hand. He looked down and met her eyes. "I'm glad you're better now, Fairy Mischief."

"Thanks, Navi. I'm sorry that you were so worried about me, but I really am fine." As he said it he realized it was actually true. Unlike when he'd used those words in conversation with his mother, he really was in a good place now. Good boyfriend, fun job, all the good stuff. "And thanks for the story, I can't wait to read it."

Freddie and the girls moved off and Link greeted the next small group of park guests.

Back in the Treehouse, Link opened the letter from Navi and carefully smoothed out the paper. It was mostly blobby pictures of what must be Fairy Mischief judging from the blue and purple body and yellow hair. He was trapped in a castle, colored with lots of black marker pen. Written in an adult hand were the words "Fairy Mischief is sad in Lord Order's castle, but he'll be okay in the end because he's the cleverest and strongest and I love him."

Link grinned, read it over again and then stuck it up on his mirror.

I'll be okay in the end. I like the sound of that.

He picked up his phone to take a photo of the letter but was distracted by a new text from his sister. She'd only sent him a few messages since the dinner. Mostly they were to reassure him that he wasn't disowned but not much more content than that.

Bianca: Hey Link, Mom just told me the most wild, amazing thing. She's going to get therapy!

Bianca: she said she might be ready to call you soon.

Link blinked at his screen and felt something loosen in his chest, some fear he'd been holding on to, some dread perhaps. If she was getting help that was a very good sign. He fired off a reply.

Link: That's amazing! OMG seriously. That could be lifechanging. How are you doing?

Bianca: you know, same old thing. How's your gorgeous boyfriend?

As if summoned, the treehouse door opened and Phoenix James came in, closely followed by Tae.

"I couldn't believe it when that whole gang of girls were all wearing Bad Fairy Coldness cosplays, I didn't know what to do," Tae said.

"Urgh, they were just the best!" Phoenix James said. "Those pictures are going to be incredible. I made sure to tell the photographer, what was his name?"

"Simon," Taeyang said.

"Yeah, I made sure to get Simon to send them through to Arlo and Lennon and Max and everyone. Those will be on the website for sure."

Link: Gorgeous, amazing and perfect. TTYL

Tae came up behind Link and kissed the top of his hair. "What's that?"

"Ah, fan mail from the youngest girl from that family we met with the biker dad and the three girls. Navi, you know? She was worried that you'd kidnapped me."

"Maybe I did." Tae chuckled. He leaned over to read from the letter, wrapping his arms around Link's shoulders and leaning on him. *"He's the cleverest and strongest."*

"Yeah," Link said, preening a little bit.

"I like that you stuck it up on the wall. Kinda reminds me of that bucket filling thing Arlo had us do. The one where you said you thought I was handsome af."

Link laughed. "I told everyone I thought they were handsome af, but I really meant it for you."

Tae let go of him, found a sticky note and a pen and wrote something on it. Link watched, his stomach filling with warm tingles. "What are you doing?"

"Filling your bucket a little more." He stuck the note up beside the letter from Navi. It read 'Gorgeous, strong, funny and mine'. Link bit his lip so he didn't squeal out loud. Instead, he got up to face Tae.

"Thank you."

"So, I take it you're having a good day?"

"Mm-hm, the absolute best," Link said. He reached for Tae's arms and pulled them around him. "And I feel like it's only going to get better from here."

- End

Thanks for buying and reading The Trouble with Order. If you enjoyed it, please consider leaving a review! Indie authors rely heavily on word of mouth and user reviews, and I'd very much appreciate it.

Thanks go, as ever, to my spouse for all their support and assistance through my publishing journey. You're a treasure and I love you.

And as ever, thanks to my two wonderfully devoted beta readers, Z and K and the new one, Timmy. Thanks team, you're excellent at weeding out the typos and noticing when I've contradicted myself.

THE FAIRYLAND SERIES BY JAXON KNIGHT

Book one: Rival Princes - a rivals to lovers romance with competing handsome princes

Book two: Mischief and Mayhem - the grumpy one, the sunshine one and a roller coaster

Book three: Recipe for Chaos - a billionaire romance, featuring instalove for the billionaire and a chef who isn't impressed with money

Book four: The Good, the Bad and the Dad - the start of a sweet menage with a single dad, a handsome prince and a mischievous pirate

Novella: Tailor Made Christmas - a second chance romance featuring a tailor and a prince, set after book four

Short story: New Year's Eve, the characters from Recipe for Chaos have a night to remember

Book five: The Trouble with Order - hurt and comfort opposites attract when Link gets a new villain

There are three golden rules for new recruits at Fairyland Theme Park:

1. No breaking character, even if you're dying of heat exhaustion
   2. Always give guests the most magical time
   3. No falling in love.

Nate's only been at work one day, and he's already broken all three.

Fast-tracked into a Prince role, Nate's at odds with Dash, the handsome not-so-charming prince who is supposed to be training him. Nate doesn't know how he ended up on Dash's bad side, but the broody prince sure is hot when he gets mad.

Dash has worked long and hard to play Prince Justice at Fairyland. Now, instead of focusing on his own performance, he is forced to train newbie Nate to be the perfect prince. Nate's annoying ease with the guests coupled with his charm and good looks could dethrone Dash from his number one spot ... so why does he secretly want to kiss him?

Fairyland heats up as sparks fly between the two rival princes. Will they get their fairytale romance before they're kicked out of Fairyland for good?

Find out in this standalone MM contemporary romance by Jaxon Knight, set in an amusement park where fairytales can come true.

Buy Now

Mischief

Protecting royalty at Fairyland theme park seemed about as far from Afghanistan as Cody could get. But the hot new rollercoaster brings up some unexpected trouble - and not the kind of trouble he knows how to handle alone.

Mayhem

Dean loves running the Spaceship Mayhem roller coaster - he gets to meet new people every day! When he sees a handsome, troubled security guard repeatedly fail to ride it, he sees an opportunity to help. And maybe they can be more than friends?

Cody reluctantly accepts cute, boy-next-door Dean's help and sparks fly between them, but between mischief, mayhem and miscommunication, can they ever make a relationship work?

Mischief and Mayhem is a slow burn, opposites attract MM sweet romance featuring snark, foolishness, motorbikes, assumptions, the chicken door and a HEA.

Buy Now

FAIRYLAND BOOK 3: RECIPE FOR CHAOS

The recipe is simple:
    Charlie cooks an amazing meal
    Charlie impresses heir to the theme park Max Jones
    Charlie gets a promotion and a dash of control over his kitchen

But the perfect recipe becomes unpalatable with one wrong ingredient and Max Jones is not behaving how Charlie expected...

Max is meant to inherit the entire Fairyland theme park but he just wants to party, have fun and bed as many people as possible. That is, until he meets Charlie and falls for him so hard he can't even finish the delicious meal.

Charlie doesn't have time for clubs or helicopter flights over the city, but Max is accustomed to getting what he wants, and he wants Charlie.

Featuring one part Billionaire, one part sensible chef, six cups of attraction, a generous dose of snark and a freshly prepared Happy Ever After.

Buy Now

FAIRYLAND STORY: NEW YEAR'S EVE

MAX AND CHARLIE GOT TOGETHER OVER THANKSGIVING - THIS SHORT story finds them a few weeks later, celebrating New Year's Eve together with Blaze and Coco, and doing some bar hopping. But Charlie's trying to find the perfect moment to ask Max something important...

An MM short story, following on from Recipe for Chaos and The Good, the Bad and the Dad.

Buy now

FAIRYLAND NOVELLA: TAILOR MADE
CHRISTMAS

https://books2read.com/tailormadechristmas/

Sparks fly and old hurts flare as two men too afraid of their feelings discover some things can't be buried. Teddy loves his job working in the Wardrobe department of a theme park, but his love life needs resuscitation.

The last thing he expected was his high school best friend and crush walking in to be fitted for a prince costume. Art wants to make it big in Hollywood, and getting a job as a handsome prince might not seem like the obvious first step, but if the rumors are true it could be the break he needs. Instead, he comes face to face with Teddy, the one he left behind.

Tailor Made Christmas is a sweet second chance romance with queer characters, set in a fairy tale themed amusement park. Guaranteed HEA. Some cursing, no cheating. This is a shorter length novella style book

SANTA'S SACKING
AN M/ENBY SWEET WITH HEAT CHRISTMAS ROMANCE

https://books2read.com/santasacking/

Darian knew from the moment Nole Ox took over BirdTalk that their ideal job writing code for a social media platform was done.

They packed up their things and went home to Snowfall, Oregon, tail between their legs for a quiet Christmas with their folks.

However, their folks want Darian to stay busy by contributing to the community so Darian finds themself signed up to help with the Christmas pageant. Thrown in at the deep end and with only days until Christmas, their only lifeline is handsome Connor, the handsome barista-turned-handyman.

Can Darian make the sound tech work so the kids have their musical cues?

Is Connor really the perfect hunk he appears to be?

And why can't Darian just sleep in?

Santa's Sacking is a sweet, tropey Christmas story that will fill your heart and tickle your funny bone. This story is Standalone but there *may* be a return to Snowfall for next Christmas...

DINNER FOR TWO

TAE'S FRIED CHICKEN

Chicken thighs
Egg
Plain flour
Panko or breadcrumbs
A low smoke cooking oil, rice bran oil is good for this
Cut the chicken thighs into bite sized pieces and rinse with water, then pat dry with a paper towel.
Break an egg (or two if you're making lots) into a shallow bowl and beat gently
Fill another shallow bowl with the panko or breadcrumbs
Put some of the plain flour into a third bowl
Roll each piece of chicken in the flour, then the egg mixture and then the panko. To keep it less messy, use a skewer to pierce the chicken as you move between bowls, or use a pair of tongs.
If you want your chicken to have a thicker, crunchier coating, do another round of egg and panko. Set each coated piece of chicken on a plate, ready to fry.

. . .

Fill a saucepan with an inch and a half, or a little more, of cooking oil and put it on a high heat. Once it's ready, put in a couple of pieces of chicken at a time and cook each side until golden brown. You can cut open a piece to ensure the chicken is cooked all the way through, it shouldn't be pink or bloody.

Set the cooked pieces on a paper towel to drain and be careful of the oil spitting at you.

Green salad with pear

Roughly chop or cut up leaves of rinsed arugula and place into a bowl, season lightly with salt and pepper.

Chop a fresh pair into slices or small chunks and add it to the bowl

Grate some parmesan cheese into the bowl, or chop up some havarti into small pieces

Add some roasted cashews or crushed peanuts for crunch

Put in some dressing, raspberry balsamic is best, and toss until everything is combined and lightly coated with dressing.

Overdues and Occultism

A witch in the broom closet probably shouldn't be so interested in a ghost hunter, right?

That Basil is a librarian comes as no surprise to his Mt Eden community. That he's a witch? Yeah. That might raise more than a few eyebrows.

When Sebastian, a paranormal investigator filming a web series starts snooping around Basil's library, he stirs up more than just Basil's heart.

Between Basil's own self-doubt, a ghost who steals books and Sebastian, an enthusiastic extrovert bent on uncovering secrets, Basil's life is about to get a lot more complicated.

Overdues and Occultism is a novella-length story featuring ghosts, witches and a sweet gay romance. It's part of the Witchy Fiction project of New Zealand authors. You can read more about Sebastian and Basil in Jingle Spells: Witchy Christmas Stories